My Own Avalon

By: Adam J. Smith

"I have loved to the point of madness; that which is called madness, that which to me is the only sensible way to love."

— Francois Sagon

It was her third birthday. Or rather, the third

year she had been attached to the form so commonly

referred to as the human body. This girl's soul was

older, much older than yours. Our birthday's, mind

you, aren't celebrated like most humans celebrate

birthdays. Their mother knew this well.

The "three year old", we'll call her Aurora, as

that is her name, was not in fact the youngest of the

sisters. The title of "youngest" belonged to a red-

head who found the body of a twenty-six year old that

stood roughly five-foot-nine was actually the least

volatile as far as "abilities" go. You see, each soul

possesses the ability to control a system of the body.

Aurora, the brain, Charlotte, the oldest sister, dark

hair and darker eyes, quiet and reserved, had the

ability to control the entire nervous system. Roslyn,

"Ro" to her sisters, the muscular system, and Fae,

who mastered the manipulation of the skeletal system at the age of ten, was affectionately nicknamed "The Puppet Master".

Night had fallen on this third birthday. Aurora stirred, fussing in her sleep. Her mother came in to check on her. Placing a hand over the child's forehead, her mother began humming a lullaby. Aurora stirred again. Her mother winced, rubbing her temple. Aurora's eyes opened, flooding with an unfamiliar darkness. Her mother stumbled back, falling to the floor. "Aurora, calm down. Mommy's here." She winced again, images of the children flashing randomly in her head as she screamed. Charlotte came running down the hall, catching a glimpse of her mother's hand. Aurora shook the darkness from her eyes and drifted back to sleep.

Dream Entry: Feb. 28, 2006

Journal Entry: Fri Sep 15, 2006, 10:34 AM

-Female Ninjas Hide Daggers In Their

Skirts And You Should Too-

Do me a favor, and just for a moment stand at the edge of your imagination. Maybe then you'll be able to grasp the plausibility of my thoughts.

Take a cluster of stars and wrap them in your hands. Be careful not to burn yourself, Lord knows; by now, you've forgotten you are still only human. Now, close your eyes and tell me what you see. And no, it isn't the darkness in front of you, look past the fact that you have your eyes closed. I thought you said you weren't human.

Now take that stone beside you and walk to the edge of the world. If of course, you can find it. Don't worry, it's there, just keep walking straight till you find it. Once you find it, have a seat, just don't look down. It's a mighty far fall for someone without wings. Remember that stone you picked up a few minutes ago? Pick out a star in front of you and try to knock it out of the sky. Go on, don't worry, they explode all the time, someone will get around to making a new one eventually. Did you miss the star? Well, the rock you threw probably landed somewhere, why not go look for it? Go on. Stand and take a step forward.

What's that? You didn't fall? Congratulations, you're a futuristic Jesus. Walking on thin air...

So, now you've sat at the edge of the world, skipped stones off the fetters of time, tried to make a star explode by throwing something at it, and walked

on the edge of the world, living to tell about it. This is

what it's like inside my head every day. And, every

night I fall asleep, there are things I dream about that

no one will ever understand because you just don't

use your imagination enough.

Dream Entry: March 24, 2006

Journal Entry: Fri Sep 15, 2006, 12:35 PM

-The Shortest Distance Between Sanity And Madness Is A Grain of Sand-

Until now, I never thought I could be so afraid of something as small as a grain of sand. Or sand itself for that matter.

You may eventually see a pattern in the world I portray in these texts. Yes, Urai was flat, but never covered in sand. Now, if you were hanging from the edge of something, wouldn't the ideal place to hang from have something under it to fall to?

Ideally, yes, however, given Urai's location, that unfortunately isn't possible. Three feet beyond the mirror you'll find the edge of the beginning of my imagination, better known as Urai, covered in a garden of various flowers crafted from gemstones

9

common to mankind. Why would you feel compelled to sit at the edge of anything, knowing that when you did there would be nothing under you? Resting your hands behind you, you feel grains of sand between your fingers. A new element to the world you hide in. And don't tell me sand isn't one of the elements. We have more than you.

In all my years of visiting Urai, I've never felt compelled to sit anywhere but on the bench or under the tree. Now, for some reason, here I sit at the edge of my imagination.

Why I would feel compelled to fall from Urai and be trapped in limbo until someone found me is beyond my reasoning, but I slipped over the edge anyway, not to fall, but to hang. Now, keep in mind that Urai is flat. And sand has never played a role here. Now you'd think I'd just climb back up right?

Don't you think I tried that?

I can't really give you a time comparison between Earth and Urai, but if I were to guess, it probably would have been 15 minutes or so before I started to slip. Remember when I told you I was never before afraid of sand? Well, when you start clawing for ground that dissolves beneath your fingers, wouldn't you be afraid of sand as well?

A quarter of my sanctuary had now crumbled to dust and the mirror that contained my thoughts had fallen to darkness. My imagination was winning a battle I was powerless to fight. The Rose Tree I had planted had been uprooted, and now leaned in the direct path of what little sun ever reached Urai. You may be thinking to yourself, "Why didn't he call for help?" Keep in mind this is my imagination. No one ever comes here. By now, Jupiter would make its only pass for the next six months...

Everything was being destroyed: Shourae itself was gone, and, in the next few minutes, its creator as well would be lost, having fallen victim to his overactive imagination....

I'm not sure how it all ended, having woke up to the sound of my alarm, the last thing I can remember was having my wings taken from me in my futile attempt to fly. The bones were cracked, rendering them useless. This would have been the fifth time I slipped...I hate sand...Someone keep me awake...

Dream Entry: May 9, 2006

Journal Entry: Fri Sep 15, 2006, 12:51 PM

Blue Tree Paranoia Part I: The Watched

(Scaring the Helpless)

How long would it take to chop down an Oak Tree if you did it branch by branch? Hours? Perhaps a day at most, and afterward, the tree lying in pieces on the ground and you, winded and fatigued, seated against the scarred stump of what used to be something wonderful. What did you just accomplish?

This, ladies and gentlemen is what it feels like when you attempt to forget what goes on inside your head. Countless times I have tried to forget, taking heed of the warnings of others, of what it would be like to be 35 and still carry the burden of an overactive imagination. Part of me doesn't want that, and part of me doesn't seem to care.

But what am I to do when half of me starts to reach out to people here... How can I have control over something that doesn't exist to others...I'm starting to think my imagination has free will, as it if were a separate host altogether...two years ago this would have been the part where I went into hiding. Retreating to what I was trying to destroy, only to prolong the inevitable of just leaving it alone. But when there is nothing left to run to, or when what you run to lies in ruin, like the tree I spoke of earlier, wouldn't that scare you? No longer having an escape from the things you couldn't control?

While asleep last night, I spent hours trying to devise a way to live without my imagination. I know after reading that you probably think I'm crazier than ever before, but not to worry, I taught my imagination how to fight back...*laughs* and you thought I couldn't control it.... last night, however, waking up twice made it quite difficult to grasp any idea that would aide me in my "search for salvation"...The forest is changing.... the trees are no longer a deep, lush green, but a brilliant blue. Blue trees? You're kidding, right? I do believe I finally *have* lost it.... Anyway, I feel like I'm being watched when I go there now.... someone has been visiting.... if you have access to my world, I beg you, show yourself.... Paranoia in the Blue Void is a very bad thing.

Dream Entry: September 4, 2006

Journal Entry: Fri Sep 15, 2006, 6:14 PM

-Blue Tree Paranoia Part II: The Hunter (Unearth the Frightened)-

I'd like to tell you I've been doing better with my lack of sleep. And most nights I have, at the expense of dreaming of course. Save for last night, where sleep came and went as it pleased...leaving me suffering from deprivation of a schedule that would provide me with enough shut eye to wake up the next morning without any trouble. Waking up three times in the passing time of three hours is not fun....

The forest is still blue. And someone has found a secure line into my head. Into my imagination, an imagination controlled by anyone except the one who owns it.... Have you ever been hunted? Not in a city, or at night. Inside your head? The forest having changed color has filled itself with traps, holes, flaws in design that threaten the nature of its creator's peaceful sleep.

The only thing I actually remember about the dream is what happened to wake me up the first time at about 3:00AM. I fell into a hole deep enough to prevent me from getting out. And dark enough to wake me with soft scream. When I fell back asleep, I couldn't see much. It was too dark in the hole to make out anything but the walls of the trap. I guess it wasn't so much the fear of being chased that made me remember it, it's the sheer fact that someone managed to get in, and stay there long enough to find me.

Bah, hunters are foolish, I'm going to bed.

Dream Entry: March 25, 2006

Journal Entry: Fri Sep 15, 2006, 7:19 PM

...Loving What Does Not Exist Will Drive You Mad

You know, I'm starting to think that being lonely is the worst feeling in the world. In the aspect of love that is, and that loving something that doesn't exist is possibly the worst thing I could have ever done. Be that as it may, I did it anyway. But what happens, when what you loved so much dies? Dies because you can no longer control what happens when you close your eyes and let your imagination take over your thoughts. Would I be so much happier having lived a life alone, or, with myself, for that matter?

Just because you don't understand anything I tell you doesn't mean you can't nod your head and actually tell me that it happened. There is a girl, who I keep seeing in every dream I have, who cannot speak, or, will not, I suppose. Covered in shadow, winged, blue eyed... The kindest, most beautiful.... figment of my imagination I've ever seen.... if someone would find me it would be a hell of a lot easier than my looking for love. I mean, honestly, if any of you could tell me where to start looking for it, I would gladly take your advice and go there. I'm probably just being a sap about not having someone of my own. But what would you do, when you can see her every night when you close your eyes, but when you wake, never have her in your arms? Wouldn't it drive you insane? Mad enough to do something as drastic as to make up a love that, let's just say, lives in Canada?

I danced with the shadow, for the first time since she caught my eye five months ago. Five months she's been haunting me, and I still don't know who she is or how I am to find her. It's somewhat frustrating...knowing deep in your heart that she is the one, but having not a damn clue as to where to start looking for her. Or, if she in fact is looking for you as well, and you should just stay in the same spot, as to not play cat and mouse with your mystery woman.... I don't know...maybe I'm driving myself crazy over not loving anyone.... If I knew who she was, this would be so much easier...

Dream Entry: May 14, 2006

Journal Entry: Fri Sep 15, 2006, 7:23 PM

Candy vs. Insanity

Is it before or after your clock has stopped ticking that you realize you are once again being watched?   Female time mages are extremely rare, but it's possible...however...there was a time, not long ago, when I would have gladly invited almost anyone with the comprehension level high enough to understand that if you close your eyes, you'll actually see there is more to the edge of the cliff than a long way down. If you don't look hard enough, you'll miss the invisible staircase leading to Staff of Ages which in and of itself is a completely different story. Or, when a boy waves his hand over a flower that has yet to bloom causing it to unfold on its own, and instead of questioning why or how, you smile, take the flower and thank him for doing what you never could....

She has returned, her eyes, however, no longer blue, but white. Now, when a human thinks of another with white irises usually the first thing that comes to mind is they probably can't see. She can see, not to worry.

Now, the second opinion would come from the human that eats candy all day and tells you that, like an airhead, it's probably a mystery flavor...

The day the iris of a human being becomes an edible object for sugar-craving children to enjoy, resulting in a spoiled dinner is the day all of us clinically lose our minds....

She calls herself Fioru.

Dream Entry: May 23, 2006

Journal Entry: Fri Sep 15, 2006, 7:33 PM

Weldin Prophecies Part I: A Boy Named Revenge

Running is something I was never very good at; I've always been slow. But when you're running from a horde of your own kind through the streets of a city that belongs to you through right of documentation and succession of rank by royal blood. And the horde is angry not at you, but at what you are...then...you run a lot faster than normal. Trust me, I should know...yes...wings are flammable... *do not* attempt to fly when running from Long Bow Fire Archers on the rooftops of Avalon.

I suppose it was about 2:00AM when I finally realized that they wanted me dead. They were arguing about my crossing over...and wanted to make sure I never made it here. This may have been a flashback, but I can't remember ever running from a horde of Angels. The tavern I ducked into after dodging a few flaming arrows was a familiar one...I knew the woman who owned the Hotel upstairs. She told me to hide in the back while she stalled them. The sun was almost up, and running in daylight from a horde of Angels was out of the question, so I tried to sleep it off until nightfall, where I would hopefully be able to get out of Avalon. Hours passed, the rustling below, on the streets outside the bar, had been reduced to a soft blown wind. I suppose now, while resting in bed, would be the best time to catch my breath and attempt to explain what went wrong...

I guess the dream started in the Council Chambers. I was arguing with Aunae about crossing over, and informing others about what went on inside my head, and how it would affect them later in life... and how if I just kept what I thought about bottled up, it would only mean my returning to Avalon. Which, of course, she didn't mind, considering; however, I told her I didn't approve of the position of my staying at all, with Yari and the children gone, she knew I had nothing left there, or Avalon for that matter. So, she got angry...And when she gets angry, she has friends... i.e. the council sitting behind her that would back her up on any position in a heartbeat. But, having been on the council before, seated at the head of the table for seven terms of office before I left Avalon for the last time, only to return on my own terms, I knew all too well that the branches of the council would follow the leader into fire without question. Thinking about it though...is it such a bad thing to let people know about what goes on inside my head? Will it really get me into that much trouble, even if they *do* understand it?

Okay, so as far as time went, I suppose it would have been about an hour before I got the okay signal that they hadn't even stopped by the bar to question anyone, so I went out the front door and just kept walking to the edge of town...that's when I saw her. Fioru grabbed my arm, and cloaked in darkness as usual, she pulled me into an alley and gave me a key. She told me the key would take me home and pointed behind me through a rundown shop. I tried to ask her what she was doing there but she pressured me to get going before they heard something.

So, off I went, into the alley...*with no door*...no key hole, nothing, the key she gave me was worthless. Of course me being me, I hadn't been through the streets of Avalon for ages, and I just stood there like an idiot, unaware of the centuries above me, positioning themselves for capture. With my back to the intersection, I could hear footsteps behind me, soft and quiet footsteps, those of a woman...they stopped just a few steps behind me and I turned to yet another figure shaded in darkness...a man, with eyes as blue as the sky....he didn't speak much.... just a few words were uttered before I was surrounded by centuries and held at sword point by Generals in my Father's Army....Generals in my Father's army? What in the Hell?

"Rie imne ishizoria lou..."

.... Yes, you've all seen this before.... any idea what it could mean? Or why the man with blue eyes would ever feel compelled to say it to me? Let alone send a horde of Angels after me? If you know, please tell me.

By now the Generals had me cornered.... in a seemingly impending doom...the hooded figure stepped forward and smiled darkly at me, removing his shroud....

"I've finally found you." I struggled to break free from the mob, only to be struck in the back of the head, and brought to my knees.... shortly thereafter, I blacked out. I don't remember what happened next.

Dream Entry: May 24, 2006

Journal Entry: Fri Sep 15, 2006, 7:40 PM

Weldin Prophecies Part II: The Broken Immortal

There comes a time in every human's life
when they realize what they fear the most and pride
themselves on staying away from what scares them.
But what happens, when what you fear resides inside
your head, let's just call it your imagination. Falling
asleep no longer becomes something you do on a
regular basis, but something you are forced to do in
fear of deprivation of what little energy you will have
when the sun rises. I should tell you that Angels
possess the same fear...or at least this one does.

Beaten to the point of retracting to the corner
of what looked to be from the sight of beaten eyes at
the "throne room," I tried to grasp the shadow of

salvation, the physical embodiment of what my dream had become. Avalon is a rich city, rich enough that assassins can buy out other assassins to do their dirty work. His name is Trega...the blue eyed man who ordered the blow to the back of my head. You see, Trega wants me destroyed...he thinks I was the one who made is father, Dunel, disappear two years ago. Now, before I continue, I should inform you that when I retreated to Shourae almost seven years ago, I filled it with things I never had here...this included a brother...and I called him Dunel...Now, before I destroyed Shourae for the final time, Dunel had left, gone missing, whathaveyou. Trega is his son. That's right folks, we're related, and he's trying to kill me.

Trega, now almost fully grown, and stronger than Dunel ever was, had a few bones to pick with yours truly...about why, and where his father was...the usual questions a worried son would ask about his missing father before pounding me into a stone wall. I suppose what little strength I had was used to tell him I knew nothing of Dunel, and hadn't heard from him in ages. This of course infuriated the boy...I believe he broke my jaw in four places before throwing me against a column of marble.... and you're probably thinking this is bad. I assure you, it gets worse...

Do any of you remember Fioru? She tried to stop Trega as I lie cowering on the floor, collapsed at the base of the cracked marble column. Removing her shroud, I caught a glimpse of her face...I knew her...from before, a past I had long stored away since Cara had sentenced her to a fate she did not deserve. Her real name is Yari, and she was my wife.... sentenced to death for high treason by my mother. I watched her die at the hands of the lackeys that waited on my mother hand and foot....

"Trega, I beg you, Cort had nothing to do with the disappearance of your father."

"You insolent ghoul, what do you know of my father!"

Those were the only words I heard spoken for I heard her scream in violent pain, having collapsed from exhaustion. I had no strength to fight that which held my life's thread between his fingertips.... And now, having stripped me of what I cherished most, he confronted me again...

"This is all your fault, mage. I will end you as you ended my father."

"For the last time, you fool; I didn't put an end to Dunel..."

I was beaten across the back with what felt like a large staff, heavy enough to break bones, and all Trega could do was laugh at me...

"I will break you, you pitiful excuse for an immortal."

Whatever Trega said after that was beyond audibility, the blood dripping from my back collected in a puddle on the floor before I was dragged to through the floor to the cells below the throne room...where I stayed for hours, collecting what little strength I had left for the next round of beatings I would receive from him.

It was then, once again that I blacked out,

lying on the floor of the cell I had been tossed into.

Dream Entry: May 28, 2006

Journal Entry: Fri Sep 15, 2006, 7:43 PM

Weldin Prophecies Part III: The Brink of Life

Sometimes, I think I was destined to lose everything dear to my imagination. And, loss is something I don't take very well. I strive to prevent it, so much so that more times than not it backfires, and I end up losing them anyway. Let's see, I lost my wife... one...two... three times... I should tell you, losing the one you love the most is the worst feeling in the world. Of course, you all already know this, I'm sure I've stated it before in one entry or another....

When I was struck unconscious before being thrown into the cell I sit in, writing to you now, I caught a glimpse of what Trega held in his hand. If you read these religiously, you've seen the words

"Staff of Ages" at least once...it alters time.... without the use of some machine with an office chair attached to it...You can carry it around, use it as a weapon; remember, it's heavy enough to break bones. And, rightfully so, the damn thing is seven feet tall...

The door to my cell opened some two or three hours later I guess, if I put together the final seconds of part two with the beginning of part three, I guess that's about right. Trega came to visit me himself.... however, this was only to inform me that Yari was no longer breathing, and that I was next. Wiping the dry blood from my lip, I stood to face him. He told me to follow him, and I did, back to the throne room where my wife lay still on the floor. As far as I was concerned, Trega had won. With my wife gone, yet again, I had no reason to be there. I confronted him for what I thought to be the last time, with outstretched arms, wanting to join my wife in whatever afterlife lie beyond that of physical death.

Trega faced me, raising the staff to my chest with a half smile.

"You're really serious, aren't you? Giving up just because she lies dead on the floor. What kind of man are you? One that puts emotion before everything else, don't you realize doing things like that will only hurt you, sooner or later?" And, with that, he swung the staff at me, striking me against the arm, forcing me to stumble to the floor. And yes, I've died in many dreams before, but I suppose the difference between them and this one is...well, I'm not sure to be honest. I guess all death is the same.

There is an edge to everything, two sides to everything...but when you are the last remaining "soul" that resides in your imagination capable of controlling what goes on inside your head, and you are faced with death. And, after death, not being able to find her...not knowing where to start looking once I wake up. For all those that are wondering, yes, Trega destroyed me...tired and fatigued, all I could do was stand there, watching Yari's body, and, before I knew it, he walked right up to me, lifted me off the ground and sent me into the floor. I had been shattered, torn apart from the soul outward, and now, lying on the brink of what humans like to call life. Trega ended my life just as quickly as he did Yari's, and we lay next to each other in the Throne Room of Avalon, Trega having finally found me, seeking out revenge for the disappearance of his father, Dunel....

Though...

What's it like to die? To protect that which you love most, and at the same time fail 1,000 times over, only to collapse at the hand of that which you swore to forget? I suppose I'll never know...

Dream Entry: May 30, 2006

Journal Entry: Fri Sep 15, 2006, 7:44 PM

Weldin Prophecies: Part IV: Crashing into Loss

For all those that believe in whatever afterlife lie beyond your physical body ceasing to function, I suppose this would be the entry for you. Not necessarily to "Heaven" some of you may believe in, but it's only one side of a belief nonetheless. Though...thinking about it now, this would probably be considered a continuation of the story I've been telling these past few entries.

After being destroyed, my soul left its physical body behind, falling for what seems like an eternity, eventually hitting a marble floor. With my truest form being more evident now than ever. My wings tattered from a fall not feasible to the human mind, and this, yet again, if you were alive, would be a fall for the winged only....

Falling for one thousand eternities only to break myself against a marble floor, I stood after regaining what little consciousness the afterlife would allow me to have back...

The voices grow louder.... The angels are laughing at the one who fell last, and the soul of the one I love is nowhere to be found...I don't wish to be alone...And it doesn't make any sense...does it...I watched her die...she should be here. Have I lost the one I never had the chance to place a physical body to? Is this the reason I cannot love? Because I can't get passed what happens when I sleep at night? At this rate, I'll never get anywhere...

Dream Entry: July 23, 2006

Journal Entry: Fri Sep 15, 2006, 7:50 PM

Yusaru Kijata: Haunted and Helpless

If you had the power to control anything, what would it be?

Ask me that question and I will tell you this...Time...and when someone lives or dies.

Of course, then you might think I was a bit power hungry, until you asked me why I chose the things I did. Instead of choosing control of my own life, or the actions of others, you are left to wonder why I would feel compelled to want to control the flow of time and gain the ability to choose when a person lives or dies. Until I then told you that the dream returned, which leaves you again to wonder what dream could have haunted me so that it would drive me to want such things as these...

Before reading the rest of this, keep in mind that this didn't actually happen, and Shourae isn't real, none of it is, I'm not psychotic, just a thinker with a imagination too big for his own good.

Her name was Lynn Winter. A girl of roughly twenty-three years of age, with more knowledge of the human shadow and it's complexities than any of you reading this. As stated in my very first entry, there was a time when I thought I could separate the shadow from the human body.

Countless tests performed on inanimate objects, toys, statues, buildings, what have you... only after I proved it safe for human contact, was I going to let everyone in on what would later torment me for what has now been several months.

When I first started working on ways to contain the shadow after separation, the most logical solution I could come up with at the time was an orb, a metal sphere roughly the size of the human fist of a thirty-year-old male. Of course, then my next task was to find a way to pull the shadow from the host. The only thing I thought of was polarity, so I went with it. Working on finding the exact opposite and condensing it into a magnet, which I placed inside the orb. The magnet was set on a pike, connected to what looked like gears to a time piece forced in the inlayed casing of the orb, causing the magnet to make revolutions, thus pulling the shadow from it's host, and containing it in the orb. After initial testing, the prototype was a considerable threat to humankind, so

I dropped the idea; the project was nicknamed

"Yusaru Kijata"-Miressian for Shadow Bomb.

And, now that you have the background of

why and how, I'll get to last night.

Imagine falling asleep and all you can hear is

someone screaming your name, not in pleasure or

anger, but in pain, loud, agonizing pain.

Running through doors, following screams of

a familiar voice, only to be stopped by a wall of glass.

The testing room, white washed walls surrounding a

white marble table.... and the screams get louder.

Don't ask me how she got there, I don't

know...

Lying on the table, her eyes the color of emeralds, laced with every amount of fear and pain a human can possess at one period of time. The bomb had gone off, laying open in the corner of the room. Her shadow was being dragged from her body, much like flesh ripped from bone. I would guess it lasted at least five minutes, and the bomb had gone off before I arrived. The glass wall was sealed to prevent contamination, the door was on the other side, and she would perish either way...

Ten minutes passed. And when all you can do is watch someone be destroyed in what your imagination believes is the most horrific way possible, you start to panic. And when she made eye contact in the last two minutes of the ordeal, I tried everything I could to get to her...

Twelve minutes was all it took. Her shadow lay in a heap, huddled around the bomb, never contained inside. And the girl, lying lifeless on the marble table. Her skin paler than that of a vampires, her emerald eyes faded, and a bit duller than before.... I sat on the floor outside the test lab, confused and frustrated...she was gone and I had done nothing at all to prevent it...When you wake up from that...what do you think it feels like? I guess it feels like having your shadow ripped from your body...not to be able to save someone...

Curse my imagination for its shadows.

Dream Entry: October 6-7, 2006

Journal Entry: Sun Oct 8, 2006, 4:08 PM

Curse the Flower, Curse the Past: The Rebirth of Zelthin

Again, forgive me for the lack of updates; I've been a bit busy lately...

This one, just to give you a time frame, is from, if I remember correctly, Thursday night, possibly Friday night.

From the looks of the people I'd say it was set in the late 1400's. Yay for traveling back in time, aye? Anyway. Judging from the accents of the villagers and the sign at the entrance to the inn, I was in Romania. (I've always wanted to go to Romania.)

Everyone was dressed in suits and big dresses. And it was dark out. A boy in the middle of the street stopped me. I proceeded to look down at him and he looked up with a soft smile and asked me why I had been crying. When I could have sworn the scars from the tears I shed the night before would have faded by now. So, I told him not to worry about it and run along, but he wouldn't go. He reached into his pocket and removed what looked to be a flower bud.

"Have you seen Shorova?"

I looked at him and shook my head.

"I'm not sure who Shorova is, but I haven't seen anyone except for you here."

He shook his head and pointed to the house behind us, it looked something like a rundown cathedral from the outside.

"Not who, what...The one you seek is in there, however."

It was then he proceeded to wave his hand over the unbloomed flower as I watched it open before my very eyes. It was white, with a soft blue hue around its pedals. He handed it to me. And pointed to the building again. So I smiled and thanked him for, at the time, doing what I never could then started walking to the building he had pointed to moments ago. The closer I got to the door, the colder the flower in my hand became, covering itself with a soft frost before closing up again. The door was big, possibly made of iron or wood, I can't remember.

Either way, I walked inside, only to be greeted by a woman of about 25 or so in physical aspects and she smiled at me.

"So, the boy has brought yet another to try and do what he could not? The one you seek is upstairs."

So, up I went into the second room on the left, only to find a room filled with a flooding darkness that crept from the window, save for the moon, which was full that night. It was then I noticed a little girl sitting in the windowsill, she was wearing a black dress, down to her ankles, resting a knee under her chin. She looked over and smiled at me from her comfortable seat at the window.

"That flower is still cursed?"

I looked at her, then the flower.

"Cursed?"

"The flower you hold in your hand is a manifestation of a past you cannot remember, or perhaps never had to begin with."

"Never had to begin with? But what about..."

"That was a past you yourself said was not your own, and now your head is clouded just like the flower is cursed and will not live. Even with the boy's help. Though, I'm quite surprised you didn't recognize him. He is after all one of your creations. Is he not?"

"One of my creations? Every male child I had perished long ago, my dear. You must have him confused with someone else."

"You mean you didn't notice his mark?"

I lifted the right sleeve of my coat and showed her the mark we all bore when born into certain military factions of my father's army. However, there were only two sons out of the three, two out of the three compliments of yours truly. Nujireu died in a sparring accident at the age of nine, thinking he was faster than me.

By this time, the boy who gave me the flower was standing behind me.

"My name is Zelthin...son of Durah and Lilith."

Dream Entry: October 18, 2006

Journal Entry: Thu Oct 19, 2006, 8:21 PM

The Seasonal Memory Coma

It's been a day. Realistically two, but I care not to count the nights I'm kept awake by a gentle forced insomnia I like to call technology. For every time I close my eyes, dreaming or not, I hear her voice. The one that sings the lullaby none of you can hear.

I've given thought to attempting to manifest the memory of what caused the lullaby in the first place, but that may only bring more confusion unto my well being. Something I don't need right now.

...

It's snowing, and, for a moment, you are blindsided by the sunlight of a new dawn as snow turns to rain and you are embedded in the core of the changing seasons. The frost that laces your memory quietly shatters and falls to a warm, gentle dust against a tile floor that holds no memory of your footsteps. Dizzy and fatigued from the defrosting of the essence of your forgotten thought, you fall to your knees, clutching your head, staring blankly at the patterns the waltzing shadows make on the floor. Your eye then catches a glimpse of a bead of sweat chasing itself through layers of time as it falls into the dancing shadows below you. Why is it so hot now? Feeling a cool breeze not seconds later as your memory flashes images of a past you are just now beginning to remember all of and it makes you shiver as you lay down, covering yourself in the shadow that stretches from your feet to the wall below them.

As you close your eyes, you wonder what the

hell you just went through....

Dream Entry: October 31, 2006

Journal Entry: Wed Nov 1, 2006, 2:01 PM

Have you ever watched something burn? Set it on fire yourself and sat in front of it, just to watch it contort and shrink, blackening and finally crumbling to a light gray ash.

And, with a flick of your wrist, you've just gained the ability to set entire cities ablaze.

A branch of elemental manipulation revolving around fire. Not because you were a pyro as a child - but because you were asked to do it. Take up the art of black magic just so you could destroy something for your creator because he didn't have the courage to do so himself.

Her name was Trinity, the second youngest daughter of the nine. Now, I wouldn't tell you I trust any of my children more than the other, but Trinity and I have ties the others don't share with me. That's why I chose her.

The very first time I opted to destroy Shourae, not realizing at the time, being so young, that my imagination would retain every memory of a past I tried to forget, I went to her. And at the time it was more of a favor than anything else. All it was, was a simple "Could you do me a favor?"

Now, before she actually went through with it, she told me that she would stay with me even if she would destroy the world she was created in. And, so she stayed, acting as what would at the time have been my first guardian angel without a physical body.

She, a gift from Durah after he created his wife Lilith, the two of which would keep watch over Shourae while I was gone. Though...it's amazing how branches of my imagination knew I would be back.

So, two days later, Avalon was turned upside-down. It was more of a fireflood, consuming the streets like a ravenous wolf. And the voracious branch of my imagination was somewhat satisfied for about a week. Until the screams of innocent shadows fell upon a slightly awakened ear. I waited two months and went back without telling a soul, to see what damage the torrent of fire had done to the city my other half had grew up in. It smoldered, with a cloud of fresh memories hanging over the break in the horizon.

Within two months of waiting to return, I had absent-mindedly started to rebuild the smaller recesses of my imagination, again, only prolonging the inevitable of just leaving it alone. Of course, equipping itself with its own self-destruct sequence called sand. It finally started to dissipate...This of course was after eight years...

Imagine having to re-live the creation and destruction of your imagination, watching everything you loved die helplessly at the hands of their creator... It's a bit painful to watch a second time.

Dream Entry: November 08, 2006

Journal Entry: Wed Nov 8, 2006, 1:54 PM

-When I grow up, I will destroy the world-

The project was simple.

Stop the world from ending. Of course, it would seem as though no one saw it coming...

Find the one that would give birth to the one that held the key to oblivion. His heart, possessing the ability to cover the world in darkness with every beat, the shadows cast onto grounds he would never grow old enough to see start to disappear, consumed by the object they are cast from. And while mankind busies itself with wondering why it's shadow is shrinking into itself, the sun is crystallizing. And every solar flare that makes it passed the coat of thickening ice sets the sky ablaze, and people start to panic.

A boy's gaze is lifted from his bedroom floor out his window as he witnesses the sky light itself on fire as the sun struggles to stay alive.

Below, the leaves on the trees turn to ash and fall to a pile below them. The trees themselves shatter like mirrors, and, one by one, the vegetation of your world ceases to function until all that is left are the hollowed bodies of the shadowless, flesh-covered containers of souls hell-bent on figuring out why.

And, at this point, the boy I spoke of earlier, born without a voice, sits on the moon and watches, a dagger in his hand; he carves into his ribcage "The silence is needed." Retrieving his heart, strings attached, he watches longingly as the world that bore him is swallowed whole by the shadows chased away from their hosts with every beat of his vital organ.

The world, now petrified and still, and the boy, taking the dagger to the dust at his feet, begins to write a letter.

"Dear Shorova,

Thy will be done. Will your heart take me back now?

Dream Entry: November 16, 2006

Journal Entry: Fri Nov 17, 2006, 3:13 PM

The Impending Fall: When water shatters bone

Suspension over a body of water large enough to drown in. Of course, you may be thinking to yourself, you can drown in two inches of water if circumstances allowed. But it was bigger than that, much bigger.

From the tip of her nose to the surface of the water below was...to be honest I haven't a clue. That's when she started to fall, slowly, with her eyes shut tight, screaming in terror as the fall seemed to last forever. For the sake of a number or possibly a mental picture, lets say 45,000 feet, from the tip of her nose to the surface of the water, and again I heard my name...

"Make it stop Eli, I beg you!"

Her eyes opened slowly; too afraid to attempt to notice when she would eventually hit the water. And, if you've ever jumped off a high dive with your eyes shut, you'll get the idea. And, for those of you that haven't heard the name Eli associated with me before, it's a bit of a long story, but just think of it as another name to call me by. I answer to it just as I would my real name.

The fall and the screaming continued. Through clouds and sky as blue as the water below her, which would soon meet her face to face...All of a sudden it stopped, everything stopped. The girl, now suspended, upside-down, roughly ten inches above

the surface of the water, her heart racing. Tears
falling from her wind-blown eyes.

Now, if I were fast asleep how am I supposed
to prevent the death of a girl, falling toward a body of
water?

...Can anyone say "Most horrific magic trick,
ever?"...

The water below her started to ripple violently
and the hair on the back of her neck stood on end,
now begging to deaf silence for help she knew would
never come. The wave came from beneath her,
swallowing her like a whale, a torrent of blue fury,
snapping her fragile body bone by bone, and the
screams continued. Begging now for mercy instead
of her life, choking and sputtering water as she

thrashed about, trying to free herself as she fought with the element.

"Eli, make it stop, I beg you! I've done nothing wrong!"

...

The screams and the struggling lasted for a few seconds longer, until a silence similar to a winter dawn crept across every recess of my imagination. The lifeless, tormented body of the girl that knew my name settled at the surface of the body of water, her hair trailing behind her. I watched helplessly as a soft breeze caressed the surface of the water. There was no movement from the girl that moments ago struggled for her life against violent torrent of water.

She knew my name...a name that few knew I had, once owned by a recess of my imagination I thought of as what some would call a father. Her hair was dark, just like her eyes: the color of Merlot, now serenely glazed over with a soft hint of fear still attached to them.

With irises the color of red wine and hair the color of the midnight sky, I cycled through my memory to try and place a name to the face of the girl I could not save, watching her be torn apart by the vicious, darker branch of my imagination.

But who was she? How did she know to call me by a name few know I will answer to?

Dream Entry: November 27, 2006

Journal Entry: Tue Nov 28, 2006, 2:05 PM

-The Unknown Fear: Shattered Glass Bones and Fading Vertical Lights-

In a room that contains no windows, a single light beams from a ceiling devoured by a familiar darkness.

Haunted by the abstraction of a memory with the power to destroy your thoughts, you watch as he dances in the darkness waiting to make his move. Taunting the streaks of darkness that pressed against the column of light in the middle of the room. Was this a way out? My escape from being devoured yet again by the strangers that kept wondering around the darker pathways of my dreamscape.

And you may be wondering why I can never protect myself from figments of my imagination, but what would you do when you are scared to move from the corner of a room possessed by manifestations of darkness capable of shattering your dreams to oblivion? He, unfortunately, had no identity that I could place, pacing back and forth on the other side of the room. It was then he collapsed, screaming in pain as he pawed at the column of light with one hand before covering his ears with both as if to try and drown out voices I could not hear. Is it possible that figments of my imagination were tormented as well?

Rage came next; you could see it in his eyes, followed by fear, and then pain. His irises were white, like violent snowstorms.

I think he blames me for his torment...yippee!

Then, he stood up, tired, struggling to stay on his feet. He started wondering toward the column of light, and his details shown brighter the closer he stepped. Intricate patterns of glass fused to his cheek bones caught reflections off the column of light softly, no sooner to be drowned in the darkness that flooded the room. Why the hell is he so tormented?

I smiled gently in hopes of calming the stranger and watched as hairline cracks split the glass formations in his cheeks into smaller shards. These formations, however, were not only attached to his cheeks...he stood again, slowly, wiping blood from his cheek and I caught a glimpse of more formations, lining the left ribcage; they started pulsing. The formations at his cheekbones cracked again and he screamed as they shattered like mirrors and dissipated while falling to the floor...He was falling apart...

Tears streamed down his face as I watched him collapse to his knees, clutching his ribs, coughing violent echoes of darkness that bellowed from his mouth, the glass lining his ribcage started resonating a soft pigment of red as they too cracked and started leaking blood, slowly dripping down his torso. With his breathing shallow, he stopped, collapsing completely to the floor as I watched the column of light flicker and retreat into the ceiling, and a woman's voice screamed my name again...

Dream Entry: November 29, 2006

Journal Entry: Thu Nov 30, 2006, 4:50 PM

-The Impending Fall: Part II: The Stranger's Aftermath

I think some would eventually be forced to classify it was blindfolded shadow manipulation.

Someone found a way to kill them, the random manifestations that wander the recesses of my imagination. And sure, I could do it, but why would I want to? As painful as it is to go through, it's just as painful to watch...Redefining my experiment to separate the shadow from its host...she uses it against them, having the same effect at the one that backfired, thus violently drowning them in their own absence of light.

She sits in an office chair in what looks to be a room almost identical to the one that held Aura captive in dotHack.//sign, minus the bed and the teddy bears. And, if you have no idea what I'm talking about, picture a chair placed in the middle of a piece of printer paper. Now, fold the paper into a cube. i.e. the rough dimensions of a room, 4 walls, a ceiling, now...collapse the walls and get rid of the ceiling so the pigment of white continues on forever and that's what it looks like.

There she sits. A navy blue, silk cloth shrouds her eyes as she lets her fingertips dance just above the armrests and random screams can be heard echoing through the vast white space around her...The lullaby continues to fade in and out, trying to drown out the screams of the horrified figments and keep me from waking.

"Everything's going to be alright Eli, I promise I'll fix everything..."

Her features were similar to the girl I had watched fall just nights before, her forearms now covered in intricate tattoos that pulsed a gentle pigment of white as her fingertips continued to dance in patterns along the armrests. The screaming stopped and the lullaby grew louder as the girl lifted her shrouded gaze above her to the vastness of an eternal lullaby she seemed to be conducting and sighed softly with a flicker of exhaustion as she stood, slipping a hand into her white leather overcoat to retrieve the a small instrument. For now, think of it as a glass Ocarina.

"I will fix it...I will fix everything Eli, just like I promised.

And, with that, she put the instrument to her soft lips and began to play the melody that kept me calm at night...

Dream Entry: December 3, 2006

Journal Entry: Mon Dec 4, 2006, 8:36 PM

**-The Impending Fall: Part III: The Second Wave:
A finished Composition-**

It's amazing what you won't do when you
watch more than one of them fall. Fall the same way
she had fallen, only into solid ground, like comets,
crashing into Earth shrouded in eternal white flames.

These two, however, survived. And, save for
their eyes, both looked just like she did. While the
dust cleared, they emerged from their holes in the
ground, wearing the same white leather coats as she,
the one with the ability to control my imagination's
death count. They, too, carried the serene instruments
resembling glass ocarinas. And when they played
theirs, she answered with hers, and it seemed to be a

79

way of them to find each other...When the lullaby was finished they pocketed their instruments and bowed their heads with soft smiles drifting across their faces as they disappeared. And the familiar falling displacement took over my body again.

Triplets...No way...

There she was, standing in front of her chair as the other two seemed to appear out of nowhere, greeting the one they had called out with a simultaneous bow, pulling their instruments from their coats they handed them over to the one with red iris and began to fade away. She smiled and shuttered softly from her shoulders as she bowed her head and sat back down. The tattoos that lined her forearms showed through her coat, no longer a brilliant white, but a deep pigment of blue. As she lifted her eyes, you could see the last pigments of maroon fade from her irises being replaced with an explosion of golden yellow. Pressing her soft lips to the glass ocarina she held in her hand she smiled at me and started to play it again.

The melody, however, was changed. Not so much different, but longer. Like what she was playing before wasn't quite finished. Flashes of light surrounded the cavity of my imagination as I collapsed to one knee in front of her, eventually being forced to the floor, the flashes of light almost blinding. But, as I lay there shivering, every flash of light causing the temperature to feel like it dropped 20 degrees. And the voices spoke up again.

"I finished it Eli. Isn't it beautiful? Sweet dreams my angel. I will keep you safe."

And she sat there, continuing to play her finished composition. Her dark hair flowing over her shoulders just as before, she had a softness in her bright eyes, to mach her voice...the kind of softness you'd find in a love, or perhaps an angel...Was she really there to protect me?

Dream Entry: December 13, 2006

Journal Entry: Sun Dec 31, 2006, 10:53 PM

**Love's Forbidden Transformation: Angelus
Erotica**

As dawn falls through your irises, you feel the
shock of a freezing explosion in the bottom of your
chest. And you are left screaming, tied to a bed, soft
velvet straps brush against your wrists as the
screaming continues. However, keep in mind that,
save for you, the room is empty. You scream for a
lost companion as light breaks through the curtains
and chases the shadows away; resting gently on your
torso, dust gently swirling in an empty storm in the
silence of the newly lit room.

She has taken your memory, and your
breath...blinking, you feel a soft breeze against your

ribcage, she has returned...sitting next to you with a playful smile she runs kisses up your torso and smiles against your ear, kissing the line of your jaw as her lips wander to meet yours. The intricate tattoo that is brandished on your left wrist pulses a gentle pigment of white as your eyes close and images dance in your head of what she'll do next. Her eyes are softer than sand...tracing her fingertips down your ribcage and sides, she runs soft kisses down your neck to your left shoulder, her fingertips passing over the newly formed bone structure resembling the root work of wings...could she be the one that made you what you are?

I'm sure it was never a goddess' intention to try and understand why. But I swear to you she looked like one...

Some say, however, that we don't start out as such...that we are made that way. She, however, was very proud of whatever she had done during her previous visit. Her long legs ran softly into her hipbones. And the soft smile she walked into the room with hadn't left yet as her fingertips continue to dance down your torso, and the feeling makes you squirm. She leans over, placing random kisses down your chest and stomach to your hipline as a sharp pain shoots through your back...the bone structure of your new form is shifting into place. The buds of the structures breeching your shoulders are starting to grow as she moans softly against your hipbone, trickling her fingertips up your sides, crawling up your body only to lay her lips on your collarbone, moaning again. Her hands resonate a gentle blue hue, much like the one the mages brandish back home when casting certain spells.

"It's almost over sweetheart, I promise..."

What feel to be a set of newly formed

shoulder blades start pulsing as they flex softly under

the muscle tissue, the buds growing what look to be

the formations of the bones of the human arm as they

drape over the sides of the bed. And for a third time

now you scream in pain. She then sits up and smiles

an all-too-familiar soft smile, her hands dancing down

your torso as her resonating fingertips leave trails of a

soft sparkle on your stomach. Leaning over you, her

lips meet your ear as she takes the lobe between her

lips and tugs at it softly, running her tongue down

your neck with a touch so soft, no human could

mimic it. Removing her from your body, she bows

gently as you are left exhausted, the framework of

your transformation laying crippled, surrounding both

sides of you as your bonds fall from your wrists and your eyes softly close. The light warming your torso recedes softly as she leans next to your ear, gently sucking at the lobe before she speaks.

"Welcome to Eternity, Cort...I look forward to seeing you again."

And, with that, she walks away, the light returning, flooding your bare torso and, again, you are left alone to ponder what she did to you.

Dream Entry: January 2, 2007

Journal Entry: Wed Jan 3, 2007, 10:41 PM

-The Impending Fall: Part IV: A Memory Flat-Lined

Would it scare you if the hand of a figment of your imagination fit perfectly with yours but you couldn't remember why? And the only reason you knew the previous statement to be true is because she saved you? Came to your rescue as your "knight in shining armor", with that familiar smile you see so often when you close your eyes at night.

Hanging in perpetual twilight, a soft haze of blue surrounds the both of you and the eyes of your mystery woman return once again. The tattoos she brandished when her other halves fell from the sky have changed to match your own. This, however, does not mean you are related, but served in the same faction in apparently at least two out of four wars in the past eight years.

Smiling, she starts to tell you of a past you struggle to remember, even the bigger details are a far cry for you to attempt to smile at. After a while, with a soft sigh at her futile attempts to make you remember her, both your hearts now beat as one. Soft fingertips grasp the chain dangling between her breasts as she smiles and lifts it to your eyes, the crystal catching a sharp hint of glistening twilight as it spun in place for a few seconds before finally halting to a stop.

"It wasn't you who draped this around my neck Eli...how did you come to grow so fond of my methods of breathing?"

"It's not a fondness, stranger...and why do you keep calling me Eli?"

"Eli is what you go by, is it not?"

"One of many names, aye. That one, however, belonged to my father..."

"Would you rather I call you something else?"

"I answer to a lot of things my dear...none of which, I'm afraid; will aide me in remembering you..."

"Not even if I called you by your birth name? Cort...you...really don't remember, do you..."

"You can call me whatever I used to answer to, I'm not sure it will make me remember you any faster, I'm sorry..."

Her eyes closed as she sighed again, struggling to understand why you couldn't remember her. Wrapping her arms around your neck she started to sing the lullaby again as tears fell softly from her eyes...

Dream Entry: January 7, 2007

Journal Entry: Mon Jan 8, 2007, 4:01 PM

-Ethcenia Grad...A messenger in the forgotten city-

The streets of the city that once belonged to you have darkened since your banishment, and the things you witnessed upon returning fall hard on the notion of the corruption created by an absent mind.

The corners of the streets your feet used to walk on are even darker than they used to be, but, by now, sneaking in and out so often, you've probably gotten used to the shadows that still dwell there.

She was just standing there in the middle of the fountain, drenched with a fog of distance about her eyes. Her hair was strait, down to the shoulders of her long coat, resembling the one your mystery woman wore after the fall. This girl, however, was younger, physically around the age of Setkai. Pointing toward you, she gently lifts her head. Blinking slowly she started to speak...

"It will change again, that symbol on your arm...I'm here only as a messenger."

"You live in the city?"

"More like hide in the city, please, have a seat."

She offered me a seat at the edge of the fountain as she stepped out of the waterfall, shaking her hair from her blue eyes. Sitting, I looked up at her as she continued to explain our meeting.

"Why are you here?"

"You didn't hear? Xevora died, you've been promoted."

"Eli's next General? What of?"

"Assassination..."

"Conflict in the system again?" I smiled at the thought of my mother's failed attempt to control what I had built. "Do you have a name?"

"Of course...they call me Ethcenia."

"After the city? Who gave you that name?"

"Mhmm, I'm Magraad Shin's daughter, Evil Grad is my birth mother...she grew up in Ethcenia as a child before moving to Avalon to join Cara on the council.... I was born shortly after your banishment and took the place of one of the scientists in the eastern wing of the capital building where I was taught the branches of white magic...now I just dabble in distortion and elemental threads."

"You remind me a lot of your mother..."

"I suppose reminding you of anyone else would be silly, would it not?"

"Yes, I suppose you're right...When will it change?"

"Whenever the one you bear now recognizes that it's not supposed to be what it is...probably while you're sleeping, no pun intended I assure you...Now, if you'll excuse me I have some work to finish back home...It was nice to finally meet you, Cort...now, go before someone sees you."

And with that she walked off down the street into a darkness I wanted only to escape...

Dream Entry: January 8, 2007

Journal Entry: Wed Jan 17, 2007, 3:27 PM

The unknown fear Part II: Shards of life

Murder usually leads to confusion and constant blame. Such is the case with most humans who usually tend to crowd around the mass huddled in a ball the base of the fountain, shuttering in pain...They stop in masses to stare at the fist sized hole in the chest of a boy no older than 16 in human years. The cavity having been set deep enough to puncture vital organs, his eyes clouded over, water dripping from his cheek. Opening his shirt, you find the same crystal formations located on the man in the room with the pillar of light, these, however, resonated pigments of soft grey and black, resembling the remains of the human shadow, which at this point had started to recede from his hands that lay stretched

97

out softly above his head. This, no human has ever seen before apparently, because it caused widespread panic throughout the crowd of maybe a dozen people, gasps of fear griping the air of the cold morning as they all huddled around the boy, again, trying to figure out why.

You're telling me no one has ever seen a receding shadow before? You're kidding right? You'd think things like this happen all the time, right? I suppose so, however, I wouldn't know, I'm not one to watch depressing television.

As dawn crests through the streets, the crowd starts to wonder what to do with the boy, his crystal formations pulsing just like before. Now, they were stirring, the resonating formations mapped throughout his body started to splinter and crack, leaking pigments of scarlet life into the streets...

In almost broad daylight, a boy collapses of unknown causes. The crystals found on his body shattering softly just before they empty completely, violent screams echoing through the shallow air, and the crowd's attention returning to the boy lying against the fountain....

That's...two...

Dream Entry: January 13, 2007

Journal Entry: Mon Jan 22, 2007, 4:25 PM

-Xiciin Jilliune: Part II: A Gift from a Memory-

Is it possible for a gap between two ledges to grow in size? At the end of the field is a cliff, with a chasm that falls forever. I suppose depth perception would cause it to look that way. And no, I didn't try to jump over it; I was just sitting there, waiting till the sun came up. Every so often, I would toss a stone into the darkness below me, kicking my feet against the wall like a child.

"You know...If you do that long enough, I bet you could fill it."

...It's been ages since I've heard her voice...

"You're late, sweetheart. What kept you?"

She smiled and sat next to me, tossing a stone at the other side.

"What will you do?"

"Who knows...I can't even begin to speak to you of distance. That just wouldn't be fair."

"Hardly, considering. I mean, look where you are now, not many can reach you here."

"I suppose I planned it that way, just in case..."

"It shouldn't be too much longer...not that you should wait or anything."

"You mean for the sunrise?"

"No, silly, ask her what I mean, she'll tell you."

I smiled and caught a glimpse of the sun; lying on my back, I watched the stars for a moment while she joined me on the ground. Moments later, the sun crested the stone wall. As I smiled, the flowers around us coiled and ignited into flames, her fingers laced in my own just like they used to be....

"Why couldn't it stay this way?"

"That's simple...you don't have a body yet."

"So, find her...I want to be with you again."

"Give it time, my love..."

She placed her hand in my own, handing me a small pouch.

"You should take this..."

"Oh, really?" I opened it, carefully dumping the contents into my hand. It was a glass ocarina, with an inscription on the side of the mouthpiece.

"Ziiju nil riem yu, ziiju nil fierria."

Dream Entry: January 21, 2007

Journal Entry: Sun Feb 4, 2007, 8:36 PM

-Xiciin Jillinune: Part III: A friendly visit

Where should I start...forgive me, last night was a bit confusing, I'm still trying to piece it all together.

The last person I ever expected to be there showed up...a Necrien crystal draped about her neck, seated against the ruins of Urai, she smiled at me, waving her hand at the thorned ruby vines entangling themselves around the legs of the stone bench beside her as they scattered slowly back into the remains of the sand that felt compelled to stay, as a small reminder of what could happen to the rest of it if I wasn't careful...

"My my, what a pleasant surprise. I never thought I'd see you here."

"Of course you didn't, I just thought I'd come to see you. It's been a while."

"You came to see me? And you needed that?" I pointed to the crystal hanging about her neck.

"No silly, I came to give it to you though...not that you need it either, but I just thought I'd return it." She smiled, standing. Pulling a petrified diamond rose from a low hanging branch of the uprooted tree, she put it behind her ear before walking to me, draping the crystal about my neck..."I brought you something, Eli."

"Oh? A present for me? Angel, you shouldn't have..."

"I know, but I found them, and knew they would make you smile." Opening her overcoat she smiled, handing me six flowers, the color of the afternoon sky. "Here you go, Angel. Those are for you."

"...Alexis...where did you find these?"

"At the bottom of that chasm you tried to fill the other day...they must have blown away before the sun came up."

"What did you say?"

"They...must have blown away? Be...fore the sun came up?"

"Xiciin..."

"Jilliune." She said with a smile. "Can we set them ablaze like the ones in the field, Eli?"

Stuttering, I sat on the bench; she followed suit, watching the twilight for the hint of sunlight that would ever reach Urai.

"Are you alright, Eli?"

"I'm...just...never mind, yes, I'm fine..."

She smiled softly, holding one of the flowers up to the dark sky, spinning it between her fingers.

"Ready?"

I smiled softly, noticing the sun cresting over Jupiter's fourth moon, watching the base of the flower flicker from a sky-blue to a ball of fire in a matter of seconds. She smiled, taking the remaining flowers in her hands, tossing them playfully upward in the path of the sunlight, watching them catch fire and explode like miniature fireworks, before falling back into her hands as a light blue ash as she looked up at me and smiled.

"I wouldn't worry about it too much, you know. You'll be alright..." Glancing at me, her irises flashed a soft pigment of merlot before she bowed and took me in her arms for a period of time that seemed to stop while we stood there. "I won't remember this you know...I don't remember a lot when I sleep, as we both know..."

She smiled again, taking my hands in her own, bowing again before hugging me.

"Good-night, Eli...sleep well."

Dream Entry: January 27, 2007

Journal Entry: Sun Feb 4, 2007, 8:52 PM

-Xiciin Jilliune Part IV: The Comfort of Angels-

There has never been a period of time when we've fought about something long enough to let the anger set in. She makes me smile, even when she doesn't mean to. Some would call it natural. Unlike how I am around a lot of people, I can be myself around her, I suppose, however, that she makes it easier, considering she is a lot like me.

"Eli, can we get more?"

I smiled softly at her.

"My, we are quite the pyro, aren't we?"

"Well, yes, but that's not why I want more. The sun will be up in a few hours, I just think it's beautiful to watch."

Smiling, I rested a hand against the base of the rose tree, softly closing my eyes.

"Eli...is something wrong?"

"Your eyes...I can't explain it, but I've seen them before."

"Of course you have, silly. I've had the same eyes forever...are you feeling okay?"

"Yeah, I'm fine."

"I don't believe you Angel, now come sit and tell me what's wrong with my eyes."

Taking a seat next to my friend of what seemed like forever, but had only been a few years, I smiled at her, trying to piece together the similarities between her and the girl who I couldn't remember.

"You see, Alexis, there's this woman..."

"Eli, before you say anything else...you know I'm not her.... I'll always be here for you, but I'm not the one you think I am. And, as flattered as I am that you find part of Yari in me..."

"Alexis, please don't...I understand."

"Eli...don't tear yourself apart over this... your forcing images into your head, I think. Trying to piece together the memory of your wife by thinking her soul resides in the body of someone you care about."

"So, it's wrong of me to think Yari is embodied in you?"

"I...Eli, I don't know what to tell you. I'm sorry."

"It's not your fault, Alexis...by any means...lest you forget it's my imagination that's tearing itself apart."

"You have to stop thinking so much, you'll hurt yourself."

"I'll be alright."

"No, you won't, you think you're going to be shielded forever...Don't be a fool Eli. Look Angel, I care about you a lot and it worries me a bit when you get this way, so stop it before I make it rain on you...."

She smiled and hugged me just as she did before.

"Thank you for coming Alexis...though...I'm not sure what I should do..."

"Just shut up and hug me, you fool. You won't do anything as long as I'm here, will you?

"No, Milady. So you can stay if you want. It would be my pleasure to keep you company while you stay here."

"It would be your pleasure to keep me at all, Eli. I can see it in your eyes, and we've been through this before, Angel..."

"You know I won't be able to just forget eight years of my life..."

"You won't have to...just try not to think about it so much. Now, can we get more flowers?"

"Maybe tomorrow, Lovey. Maybe tomorrow."

Dream Entry: February 3, 2007

Journal Entry: Thu Feb 8, 2007, 8:59 PM

Go to a city...any city with buildings that seem to reach the sky...New York, or Los Angeles for example. Now go to the roof top of one of the sky scrapers, you'll see a man waiting for you, think of this as that scene from City of Angels. Only there were no conversations between two angels per se...

Fallen from the sky, the pupils of the man you met on the roof dilated to the point of obliterating the whites of his eyes. Which, if you've ever seen the movie "The Covenant," You know what it looks like, or even the preview where they "jump the gorge." Anyway, back to the story...

The sky was getting brighter, the closer you walked to the huddled mass on the roof. His entire body shuttering, as it he was covered in snow.

"Don't touch me...I'm not done...not finished, don't touch me."

Flashes of shadow in the sky above the building you stand on cause the man with darkened eyes to scream violently.

"I said, don't touch me!"

Blinking, the man in pain begins to cry, as you struggle to figure out whom he's talking to.

Clawing at the glass roof, staring blankly at the brightening horizon, the man screams again.

"Why won't you let me finish it!"?

The veins that ran through the length of his arms and upper body filled quickly with blood, bulging slightly against his muscles.

"Don't touch me, you fool, you don't know how it works!"

Waving his hand at the space in front of him, the blackness in his eyes began to pulse and swell, his fingertips drawing intricate patterns against the horizon only causing the flashes of shadows to collect overhead as an ornamental staff, heavy in weight and longer than usual blinked into existence, adorned with eight crystals set in an ancient formation maybe only a dozen would recognize. Gripping the staff, with his eyes fix on the brightening sky, he smiles at you and collapses again.

"I told you...I'm not finished yet...I'm not..."

The darkness in his eyes begins to fade as his grip on the staff loosens until he finally drops it on the roof. A few seconds later everything stops. The illuminated sky continues to flash patches of shadows as the staff now lay out in the open for anyone to take.

Walking up to it, you wrap a cautious hand around the base and raise it to the horizon, just as the man had done. Upon aligning the crystals with the correct pattern of light, you blink out of existence, taking the staff with you.

Reappearing at the foot of a staircase lined by while crystal walls, guarded by hooded soldiers bearing crystals embedded in the palms of their dominant hands, you now stood in the presence of Avalon's most powerful guards, at least at the time.

Shortly after your arrival, a young woman at the foot of the staircase greets you as you drop to one knee, bowing in great respect, for before you stands the guardian of the Staff of Ages.

With no relation to any of the royal family, the guardian appeared on the steps of the shrine some months before the completion of the staff. She, a young girl at the time, cloaked in shrouds, adorned with a single "trinket" about her neck.

This trinket, crafted from crystals formed from shattered stars caused by the wars of the ancient ancestors of the royal family.

She, having never given her name, was deemed simply..."Mithilil" (which, to all that do not speak Miressian, means Guardian.)

Presenting the young woman with the staff, you rise, backing away from the staircase as she begins to make her way to an alter where she would lay the staff and turn to the woman seated to her right, bowing in respect before taking an oath in a language none of you reading this would understand.

She was later given the title and name change of "Riij, Guardian of Ages."

Dream Entry: February 15, 2007

Journal Entry: Sat Feb 17, 2007, 9:04 AM

-Dear Diary, let go of my stardust lover-

A woman stands under an oak tree in the midst of a rainstorm, one foot resting comfortably against the trunk and her hands placed delicately against the pages of a book some hundreds of pages long. Soft-spoken ancient tongue slips from her mouth as the pages flip back and forth and the rain falling from the sky ignites against the treetop setting the leaves ablaze.

This classic book form of elemental manipulation was practiced in early times until more convenient methods were thought of.

A key, molded from an Aziir shard, dangles from a cord about her neck, probably the key that opens the book. Think of it as one of the most intricate diaries ever kept.

Blinking softly, the rain subsides, crystallizing into purified stardust at her feet...and from the stardust unearth the fingers, hand and soon to be entire body of a man standing just over five feet in height, deep green eyes, his back scarred between the shoulder blades, a scrolling tattoo adorns his right arm, the fact that he was built well was evident by his muscle structure, though that plays little part in the story.

"I can't hide you forever, my love."

She kissed him softly, smiling as her eyes wondered to the sky again, the rain dripping from the smoldering treetop. Unable to speak for the moment he smiled back at her, bowing his head. Glancing at his tattoo, the man turned his palm to the sky, watching the patterns shift like clockwork machines. Embracing her, he whispered softly in her ear.

"Come with me."

Smiling against his neck, she shifted her gaze from the remains of the stardust to his eyes.

"We've been through this before, I can't..."

"But."

"Shh, don't waste your energy. I'll see you again, I promise."

"Aye..."

Backing away, into the rain after kissing her again, he dropped softly to one knee, as the girl turned back to her book, placing her hand over it again. Tears began to fall from her eyes as she watched the man she loved start to dissolve from the fingertips upward and then back down to the gentle hue of the stardust that bore him...

Dream Entry: February 22, 2007

Journal Entry: Sat Feb 24, 2007, 11:18 AM

-The Impending Fall: Part V: Prelude to the fall

About twenty miles off the coast of Tameril, which resides south of Avalon, just through the Zarthal-Ren Woods, (when I say woods, it's big enough to be a forest) rests a cliff set against the Jiir Mountains. Here, at the cliff's edge, sits a woman reading a book, her fingertip running lightly down the pages as if to search for something. Her white long-coat had fallen from her shoulders, and her dark hair was pulled to one side, resting on her right shoulder.

Smiling softly, her finger resting against text of the ancients that wrote it, she began to recite what was written, speaking soft and fluently against the gentle wind that accompanied her on the mountain.

Closing the book, she took a glance at the water below her and then stood. The air today was thinner than usual. Struggling to inhale for a second, she looked up at the sky as if to ask for help before backing away from the edge. Placing one foot in front of the other, her fingertips began to dance along layers of air as the shadows cast on ground around her began to collect at her feet. After completing the primitive ritual, she set the book down and began walking to the edge of the cliff. Then, continuing with cautious steps, she placed one foot on thin air over the edge of the cliff. The shadows that had collected at her feet rippled against air currents and formed what looked to be somewhat of a "magic carpet" beneath her.

Continuing to take steps forward, she glanced back at the book she left behind, turning back around, she continued on, walking out over the water,

standing some hundred thousand feet about the

surface, or at least so it looked to the naked eye of an

on-looker from the beach.

Oblivious to the dissolving shadow

surrounding her feet, the woman stopped, looking up

at the sky. Retrieving an instrument from her coat,

she put it to her lips and began to play it. Her legs

shortly thereafter began to tremble, losing the support

of her manipulation, she winced softly, a soft fear

coating her eyes as she pulled the instrument away

from her lips.

Seconds passed, and the collection of shadows

at her feet continued to dissipate, causing her to

slightly lose her balance.

"No, not now...I'm only trying to help him!"

Slipping from her manifestation, screaming blankly against the sky, she tried to cling to whatever remained of her shadowed carpet...It was then that she started to fall. Screaming again, she managed to utter a sentence, laced with every ounce of fear a person could possess at one time.

"Eli! Eli I beg you, make it stop!"

Dream Entry: February 28, 2007

Journal Entry: Thu Mar 1, 2007, 4:53 PM

-Into the Darkness: Goddess of the Stone Flower

The walls formed around the outskirts of thought are built to keep people out and thoughts in.

The gap looks even larger than before, and I've been meaning to record the tune that keeps my demons on their leashes...I know what's at the bottom...A lake filled with the stones I had tossed at the other side that night, and the flowers that would scatter and blow off the edge of the cliff when the sun rises. Beneath the water rests a woman (please, no lady of the lake jokes...).... She was far from that description. Her eyes were bright, glowing a gentle hue of silver in the darkness she housed herself in, watching as her fingertips breached the surface to clutch a fallen flower, only to petrify it into stone and chase after it as it sunk to the bottom to join the thousands of others that had fallen into the water.

I felt something in my head scream at me as she arranged them carefully on the lakebed. I didn't have enough time to ask her why. She was gone in a matter of minutes.

I found one she had forgotten, picking it up; I twirled it between my fingertips, smiling softly at the memory of her.

The voice started to scream again, a violent tongue only I would understand. It would seem the voracious branch of my imagination was lashing out again, hungry for thoughts I couldn't begin to describe to you.

Interrupted suddenly, once again by the
lullaby as it only got louder, drowning out the
begging for memories, shouting of don't forgets and
come back home's. Clutching my temples, I collapsed
again, watching her return for the flower she forgot,
taking it entirely in her hand, swimming back into the
darkness again as I lay there, soaked and
stunned...eyes glazed over in a haze of comatose, the
lullaby dancing in and out of each ear.

Journal Entry: Wed Mar 7, 2007, 7:30 PM

Ramblings of a sleep deprived angel.

When you close your eyes and mass confusion begins to spread from one side of your dreamscape to the other, and echoed screams of shadows you can't remember get louder as the seconds pass, causing you to toss and turn in a sleep that is limitlessly futile, who would you turn to when you woke up?

...

I remember what it looked like before that day.

You, among a few others, would never be able to comprehend why or how I would come to create something such as my garden, but I remember every

133

detail...I digress, however, for last night I sat at the edge of my newly formed state of thought....

It's colder now...much colder than it ever was, despite the lack of sunlight...To be honest, it just feels lonely now. The remains of the destructive element have scattered itself across the surface of my sanctuary, as a way of reassuring me that things would stay that way for quite some time...

They've grown back...my tattered gift, given to me by the goddess I couldn't seem to remember. The scars from the shifting bone structure have faded, though I'm still getting used to the fact that something won't let me let go of it.

Brilliant white feathers brandishing soft golden hues at the tips have replaced my broken frames. The wingspan itself hasn't changed much, which Cara used to love to call "The Guardian's Wings"...which makes sense, I suppose, given my thought process over the years....

Is it possible to have an anniversary with yourself? Or is it true that I think too much...

It was mid-march when I was married to her, five years ago...March 19...who knows why I let myself remember that...I wonder what I'll do when that day arrives...

I miss her...is...that wrong of me?

Dream Entry: May 28, 2007

Journal Entry: Wed May 30, 2007, 9:32 PM

-Weldin Prophecies: Part V: The Letter: Of gifted keys and burning flowers-

There is a place among the stars where you can watch flowers burn as the sun rises, and sand flow softly against the absence of gravity...

I should tell you; I miss you more so now than the first few days without you. Why must I be haunted by your eyes? Have I no escape from the love I cannot find to begin with? Or perhaps the love that has yet to find me. For I should stay put as to not play cat and mouse with your physical body.

If what doesn't kill you only makes you stronger, what happens when it stings just enough for you to sit at the edge of the world and rearrange the stars in hopes that she will notice.

I miss you...in every aspect of the phrase, I miss you. And, I'm sorry. I know you probably don't wish to hear apologies from me, but it's always after the fact that I think I could have done something more or perhaps something different. I found your letter...and I am sorry...Quite a hiding place for such a letter my dear, I must say...but why?

You took the blame for me...for my experiment.

Cara thought you were the threat...

I can't begin to apologize, for a few things, mostly not being there...Cara called it treason. But all you wanted to do was protect me. Love, I'm sorry. It wasn't supposed to end this way...not at all...I wish to see you again...I'll keep your key safe, I promise...

...

My Dearest Cort,

By now if you are reading this the key around your neck no longer has a purpose, and I am once again torn from the one I hold closest to my heart. I apologize for never telling you who I was...If I was ever discovered, well...I'm sure you know. Allow me to take this time to explain why Cara did what she did...

After the accident in the lab, word got out about Lady Winter's death. Cara's generals would start questioning everyone in affiliation with her, myself included. You, however, were conveniently shadowed from all the interrogation due to your lack of sleep. They had no way of getting to you, and Cara dare not bother with the petty details of asking her son if he had anything to do with it, trusting that you would never do such a thing. That day, they came to the house asking about the accident, I simply smiled and told them it was my idea. What Cara labeled Treason was actually unstable murder, but she didn't want panic. And who could blame her. My love, I am truly sorry. I will see you again, I promise...know that I love you with all my heart and will be waiting to hold you again when the time comes. Be safe my love, I will see you again.

Vaira yer Cestilen,

Yari

Dream Entry: July 23, 2007

Journal Entry: Wed Jul 25, 2007, 1:16 PM

Dear Diary Part II: Imprisonment of Shadow Manipulation

The screams had stopped, and the rain that fell above the forest she hid in could no longer be felt.

Bowing before her, the love she summoned before rose to take her hand.

"They know about the book, Lucian. Now they hunt us both."

"But I am the one they want..."

"And I am the one that keeps you safe..."

141

"We must fight."

"Or die trying. Lucian, are you insane? Two against an army? A Legion of armed soldiers who all know your secret...your weapon is no good against them."

"Or die trying...I won't be trapped in these pages forever, let me fight. If anything, I may at least be able to save you."

"Damn it Lucian, I won't lose you again! Lucian don't do it!"

Those words fell on deaf ears, as her love began to vanish just as before. Without protest, she followed, both appearing under the tree again.

It was during that time that the army she spoke of had uncovered the book's location...

As Lucian walked toward the front line, tears began to fall again.

"Lucian don't, I beg of you!"

Her love's eyes had faded to black, as one of the men at the front line began to speak.

"Lucian Orune, you are charged with the murder of..."

With a smile, Lucian raised his hand in front of his chest, spreading his fingers as the soldier's shadow began crawling up his legs, pulling him beneath the forest floor with a violent scream.

Encasing himself in his own shadow, Lucian began to eliminate the soldiers handfuls at a time. With his love standing behind him, forcing back her tears, she watched the tattoo on his arm shift slowly.

Finally managing to flank the couple, a mob of soldiers struck the girl from behind forcing her to her knees.

"Niirumi! Don't you touch her!"

Turning to face the mob, Lucian screamed violently, waving his hand at every soldier cornering his love, watching them panic as their shadows were pulled from their bodies, collected by the forest around them. Rushing to her side, he tried to mend the wounds of his love as she began to speak.

"Give them what they want..."

"Niirumi, please don't go..."

Closing her eyes, Niirumi curled up in Lucian's arms, her heart slowing to a stop as the tattoo on Lucian's arm shifted again. Moving his lips as if to speak he was met with silence. Once again, his voice had vanished, a result of the clockwork tattoo on his arm.

Screaming a harsh silence, tears began to fall as he held his love in his arms, she still clutching the book. Taking Niirumi up in his arms, he stood to face what was left of the army behind him as one of the generals stepped forward and started to speak.

"If you're finished here...we'd like you to come with us."

Holding back tears over his fallen love, Lucian followed the army back to the Great Hall without much more of a fight.

...

"And just how did you manage to get out?"

Keeping his eyes fixed on the floor, Lucian could not answer. A hooded woman stood from her seat at the head of the table in the back of the Great Hall as Lucian struggled against the guards, screaming again in harsh violent silence, a few tears falling from his eyes.

"Drown him in text..."

Being forced to his knees, Lucian struggled to break free from the soldiers, screaming repeatedly, only to be met with the same harsh silence as before as two hooded figures stepped in front of him, placing their hands out in front of them, their palms facing his struggling body.

Reciting more of the ancient text Niirumi had used to bring him back from the book, Lucian watched as the fingertips of the sorcerers obtained a gentle shadowed hue, and he continued to struggle, trying to escape a fate he hoped to never see again as panic set in and a soft haze of fear clouded his eyes.

Watching helplessly, he noticed the book wrapped in Niirumi's arms had fallen open to random pages somewhere in the middle, and his struggling

continued, getting more violent and fear stricken as

the seconds passed. He winced softly, struggling to

prevent the inevitable, blinking softly with hope of a

small retaliation; the shadow of one of the sorcerers

wavered gently, starting to crawl up his robe. The

hooded woman behind the table smiled gently at his

efforts to stay "alive," nodding to one of the soldiers

holding him down.

Arching his back in pain, Lucian screamed

once again in silence; the guard smiled and knelt

down behind him, pulling his dagger from Lucian's

shoulder as the shadow of the sorcerer settle down

again and the ritual continued.

The now horror-stricken eyes of the shadow

weaver noticed his fingers and hands begin to

dissolve, falling like dust onto the empty pages of the book at his knees. Watching, struggling as he was helplessly torn apart, while what was left of him started to read the text translated by his body onto the pages of the book. Wincing again as the magic devoured the tattoo on his arm, working its way through his entire body as if someone were unraveling a sweater.

With the tattoo gone, Lucian's voice returned, letting out the most agonizing of screams, as the spell climbed his neck and the rest of him finally disappeared, his scream fading as the text in the book finished writing itself.

Smiling gently, one of the sorceresses waved his hand at the book, closing it as she was greeted by the hooded woman who, with a smile picked up the book of the floor and moved to Niirumi's body,

pulling the key from the chord about her neck with a

gently snicker of amusement. She locked the book

and dropped the key in her pocket, placing the book

in the empty space on the shelf next to her.

The guards bowed gently and carried

Niirumi's body away...

"That's the last of them..."

Dream Entry: September 5, 2007

Journal Entry: Thu Sep 6, 2007, 9:33 PM

Yusaru Ceravoria: What I wouldn't give to have her back...

It's been a while since a nightmare has stuck with me in such a way that I wake up fear stricken the following morning, having slept through the entire thing. Though, you may ask yourself how many times can one person be haunted by the same dream? As much as I'm sure you'd love to hear the story of the shadow bomb again, this nightmare was different.

After Yari was convicted of treason, she was taken to Avalon's Great Hall to be dealt with the same way Lynn had suffered.

Most of the mages who resided in the Great Hall knew a thing or two about shadow manipulation. Four of which were volunteered by Cara to carry out the execution, believing the notion that you could not live without your shadow. And though most or all of those that read these entries religiously have read the letter and know how Yari died, this is just to give you a different perspective, considering how I saw it...

...

Yari didn't say much, only struggling when she felt it was needed before the mages began the execution. To be honest, I'm not even sure she was afraid. She knew how the experiment worked in the lab, and what it was meant for; however I don't think anything could have prepared her for the pain she would endure...

152

Bound to a wall by cuff and link, her soft blue eyes blinked at the floor as members of my mother's council began to enter the Great Hall, seating themselves on either side of their leader, followed by a select few witnesses, among them were our daughters...Faith, Hope and Setkai...all of whom sat in the front row of the gallery as a soft smile crept across Yari's face, noticing her children take their seats.

Setkai, the youngest of our children stood seconds after taking her seat next to her older sister Faith, gripping the wooden railing of the gallery as she made eye contact with Cara, shouting a threat through falling tears at the one who would destroy her mother, as she was wrapped in Faith's arms and told to be quiet.

"Rie imne ishiizoria lou. Lou zotsaiku vorden..."

With a smile, Cara nodded to Setkai as the entire room fell silent and the mages stood to face the convicted, their fingertips already having obtained a gentle shadowed hue. With her executioners in place, Cara began to speak, paying no mind to the threat of the child in the front row.

"Yari Manaka. You have been convicted of High Treason, on the grounds of Unstable Murder, and threat to society. Your Sentence for such crimes is death, by the style of the council's choosing."

Looking each of her children in the eye, Yari struggled in her bonds gently, as one of the guards nearby shoved the butt of his staff into her ribs, ceasing her struggle, causing her to cough and wince in pain as Cara continued with her speech. Yari's three remaining children would have been the only family witnesses, save for their grandmother Cara; I at the time, was preoccupied with the destruction of Urai.

"The council has chosen your execution, and the gallery shall watch you die the same way you killed Ms. Winter..."

Struggling again, the mages volunteered to carry out the execution began reciting an ancient text from memory as a shadow of Yari's body that stood against the wall behind her began to ripple softly, shifting downward slowly as her shadow began to crawl from her body. Tears welled in her eyes as she struggled, holding back screams of pain as her shadow shifted from her body. Within a minute or so,

her struggling became more violent, trying to prevent

the detachment of her absence of light, screaming in

pain as she threw her head back and lashed about

against the wall.

Most of the Gallery was comprised of select

townsfolk and High Mages of Avalon, these of which

couldn't bear to watch a woman in such pain...most

shielding their eyes, or turning away and covering in

their ears as the screams echoed through the Great

Hall.

Whimpering between screams of pain, Yari

thrashed about against the wall, the color draining

from her entire body as her shadow collected at her

feet and receded to the fingertips of the mages that

stood in front of her. Just like the night Lynn had

suffered so greatly...it only lasted a matter of minutes. Yari's screams lingered through the Great Hall after the mages that stood in front of her dropped their hands to their sides, the shadow of the convicted collecting in their fingertips.

Cries of sorrow fell from the lips of all three of her children, Setkai's eyes frosted with rage as tears fell down her cheeks. Swearing to herself that one day she would find me again...and inform me of the things that had happened.

A public execution has happened only once in the city of Avalon...

Yari Manaka...convicted of high treason at the age of 159 on the grounds of unstable murder and threat to society.

I wonder now...would things have been

different had I been around to take the blame for my

own experiment...could I really have been able to

save the one I love...

Dream Entry: December 12, 2007

Journal Entry: Thu Dec 13, 2007, 10:40 PM

Ramblings of a Sleep Deprived Angel II: An update for the masses

I suppose after three months of silence I owe those that read these entries avidly or otherwise somewhat of a lengthy update. And I thank you all for your interest, and apologize humbly, for the aftermath of my wife's death has left me a little less than dreamless these past few months.

...

What remains of my sanctuary has been rebuilt, the tree replanted, as well as the garden. With the help of Setkai in Eli's absence who at the time was away on "business", but I'll get to that in a minute. I'm still toying with the idea of piecing the mirror back together, but I really haven't come to a decision about that yet. Not sure if I want to witness what happened to Shourae after the mirror shattered.

But I've been sitting under the tree, watching the roses bloom again, come February it'll be fully-grown again. A few weeks ago Eli returned from his trip, a bit of a favor for yours truly.

Travel to Avalon and find the Staff of Ages, no matter its condition return it to me, for I had this notion on my head that I could still save her...

I know it's been a while, but I'm sure most, if not all of you, remember the Staff of Ages, remember what it does, how it works, and who killed Riij to get it.

Yes...I'm sure most of you remember Trega...I'm still not sure what he did with her body after he destroyed me, but if I had the staff, knowing what it does, I might have been able to go back and been there the day Cara's generals showed up and my front door, questioning my wife without me there. And I'll admit I was quite excited about the idea, until Eli returned with the staff.

The staff itself is comprised of eight crystals at the head, embedded in an ancient formation laid out by its creators, however, some of you might remember when Trega confronted me in the Great Hall after Yari's death... when he struck me down with the staff. In doing, so he splintered two of the crystals, causing the fractures of light to shine differently against the horizon which presents a few problems to anyone that would attempt to use the staff for it's true purpose.

And, to be honest, there are a few who think doing so is wrong, for a few reasons. Though, a few months later, after seeing her apparition a few times, I was tossing the idea of going to war with the one that started it all around. That's right folks, I had given thought to going war with my mother, Cara. At this point it's a foolish move, considering, due to my banishment, I'd have to ninja my way back into Avalon to even have access to her in the first place. On top of that, she has an army, something I lack ever since I was stripped of my rank after being banished. So, if I am to challenge her at all, I'd have to build my armies underground and come at her from above, but, as I said before, there are those that frown upon the idea of losing me to my imagination, and strive to keep me here...

So, for now, I wait, quietly stirring in my sleep as the stars explode around the moon and the gentle breeze of the human's outer space greets my cheek with a cold hello, offering the few grains of sand that still stir themselves about the surface of Urai...

Not really sure what happens now...I guess...I wait.

Journal Entry: Wed Dec 26, 2007, 10:45 AM

An update for you, yes, just for you.

To those that are worried about my going to war...The following message is for you. I will not go until I am prepared enough to win. If I planned it right, come February, when the roses are in bloom is when I will take my armies through the mirror. For everything I'm fighting with, aside from my daughters and possibly Eli, who, at this point, will probably stay out of the war, considering his position, (For those that don't know, or don't remember, Eli is Cara's Husband. She left him when I was just a child for one of his generals in training, who she later banished to what were, at the time the "cursed woods" of Zarthal'Ren.) Is expendable, conjured if you will. And to those that wish to go with me, I am sorry, but this is a war I must fight alone. Unfortunately, only a handful of you have an effect on what happens to my imagination. All of whom, I'd guess have no idea what's going on. I've been asked by a few what effects this war will have on my physical state, and, I assure you, those that don't know about it won't be able to tell the difference. I refuse to bring it up unless someone asks about it, not wanting to cause too much confusion for those that don't need to know why or how, or even the history of basically everything that went on in the past nine years.

And, not to worry, I'll keep you all posted; half of me will stay here to keep my physical self-active enough that he looks like he's still alive. I suppose the good news would be I wouldn't leave until I'm ready; if that happens to be later than February, then so be it. At the earliest, however, that's when I'll finally get to see what happened to Avalon after the mirror fell from Urai, shattering against the stars.

...

And to those that told me going through with this would only end badly, and, in turn, didn't want me to go through with any of it, the more sensible side of me will apologize for the side that's actually going through with it. As I've told so many that were worried about losing me, I won't walk through the mirror until I'm sure I can come out alive. There's not really any point to it...Until I have the chance to write again, I wish you all the best.

-Cort Taenvir

Journal Entry: Mon Dec 31, 2007, 2:28 PM

Babble, babble…Xiciin Jilliune

Welcome to a closer look at my sanctuary; better known to those that read these entries religiously, or at least keep up with them, as Urai.

Believe it or not, Urai was created first. A meteor set in orbit around Jupiter's fourth moon. Flat, yet long enough to not see the other side with the human eye. At one end, there is a garden of earthen gemstones grown into flowers found on various parts of earth. In the middle of the garden, as most of you may already know, grows a tree of diamond roses. However, at the other end, lay a field that runs to the edge of a cliff set deep to the core of the meteor and at the bottom, rests a lake where what little sunlight that ever reach Urai dare ever travel. The field itself is comprised of small blue flowers, rimmed in a soft

167

cream color. When the sun crests over the cliff's edge,

the base of every flower turns a brilliant white,

heating themselves to the point where the petals set

themselves ablaze, setting off a chain reaction, and

thus igniting the entire field, a light blue haze of

smoke the scent of lover's souls fills the air as the

blue dusted ash falls to the meteor's cold soil and

within the next twenty-four hours grows back into the

same phenomenon affectionately named Xiciin

Jilliune, also known as Fire Flower.

Journal Entry: Thu Jan 10, 2008, 9:58 AM

Promises Promises: The fear of Loss

Ask me what I fear the most...go on, read the subject. The loss of someone I care about. Despite the fact that if she were to follow me into the depths of my imagination, and hunt me down only to drag me back before I do anything too drastic, she could probably hold her own. I do not wish to lose her to what I might not be able to control, or not see coming. For now, we'll call her Raiya.

I should tell you she's the only one that threatened to chase me down if I went to war. Granted, there are those select few that said given the choice they would stand with me when I go up against Cara. But I've already lost someone I care about, more than once mind you... I don't wish to lose

169

anyone else, especially her...And, if the war happens, I won't be there, more than likely a branch of my imagination will take revenge on another out of sheer hatred for the other, thus starting a war without me involved. Which honestly could very well happen. Considering Setkai was forced to watch her mother die. Personally, I don't blame her. But I'm not sure if she'll go through with it or not without me there. I guess only time will tell, aye?

So, I suppose this entry is for you Rairai. I think I'm finally starting to realize how lucky I am.

Cheers Darlin'

Dream Entry: January 14, 2008

Journal Entry: Tue Jan 15, 2008, 9:40 AM

-The Impending Fall Part VI: Ziiju nil riem yu, Ziiju nil fierria

In the dark and broken recesses of a city scorched by magic, the promise of a forgotten memory returns to haunt the still whispers of a once peaceful sleep.

"Sleep well my angel, I will keep you safe."

You know, it's funny, I still don't know who you are... and your method of breathing proved quite useful in the early stages of my creation. For those that don't know what it is I speak of, the woman I can't remember seems to have, shall we say "invented" the Necrien Crystal, or charmed it in such a way to make it work the way it does.

The trinket that a few have draped about their necks to aid them with breathing on Urai...

She seemed so sad, the last time we spoke. That I couldn't remember for the life of me who she was. She never did give me a name. Though she knew mine, so well, in fact, that she knew almost every name I've ever answered to. And, to have the ability to sing a lullaby that keeps my demons on their leashes long enough for me to obtain an ample amount of sleep at night, is quite a talent, I must say.

She has returned, and with her, the lullaby...Yari gave me the instrument she uses...if, in fact, they are intertwined, knowing that would make this a whole helluva lot less confusing. Or hell, even if she would just tell me her name...I only knew a few of the folks that lived in Tameril when I was growing up, my memory could be full of gaps, considering all that has happened. And if, in fact, you are now wandering the ruins of Avalon in search of the one you claim to love so dearly, I'm not there... you'll have to look elsewhere.

For the sake of keeping my sanity...tell me your name.

Saturday, January 26, 2008

The Impending Fall Part VII: The Walker,

Banishment of a Creator

What would you do if you were told the one that keeps you asleep at night was a creature bred by seduction?

The one I can't place a name to has taken refuge in the shadowed recesses of the ruins of Avalon and now, given the opportunity, I must force her to leave.

An outsider, a wanderer that preys on the weak, known to some as a succubus. The creature that kept its mouth shut when offered the chance to give me a name apparently doesn't own one. But how am I to fight with a means to kill something if it will

174

not die? To drive away what only wishes to "help me."

It has gone into hiding or else I would have confronted it two nights ago, which leaves me forced to find what apparently already knows what I know. And, I should tell you, incubus or succubus, I may actually need help with this one.

. . .

We call them walkers, those that come from the outside, having nothing to do with us in any way, shape or form, no pun intended. You know it's funny; she bore a slight resemblance to Yari, even after first glance. I suppose that's partially why I paid no mind to the fact that she may have been out to harm me.

But again, how do I kill what cannot die? Or

perhaps refuses to go away because it believes it's keeping me happy. And yes, I know, I possess abilities far beyond that of most, but lest we forget those that may have survived the mirror's fall still have a job to do. I'm not sure how much detail I went into before, if any, about why I was banished, so I suppose now before I return would be a good a time as any.

. . .

It's been almost three years since the meeting with Aunae and the rest of the council. And granted, banishment turned more into my getting chased down rather than asked to leave for good, but banishment is banishment no matter how you slice it. And no, Trega was never put on the council, even after he came of age, at which point he, too, went into hiding until he had enough mind to hunt me down the next time I would return to Avalon for any reason.

It's what we call "crossing over," branching out to those in a world that will never understand yours. Sure, you could say they feared for my safety, or perhaps more so their own, but it was either one or the other with Aunae. And, even my mother, who refused to get involved at the time, would have told me the same thing had she been put in such a position. And not to worry, I won't rewrite the entire sequence of events leading to Yari's second death. Those that remember any of the Weldin Prophecies will know what I speak of.

After the one I named the goddess brought me back to life, I took refuge on Urai, and waited for years until things died down a bit. The day I went back with the key Yari had given me was the day I found the letter hidden in a blank picture frame with a keyhole in the center.

Stay in Avalon, or return to Earth, a simple choice

really, why would one choose to leave in the first place you may ask yourself? Trust me, I had my reasons. Since there was no in between, I was hunted. That's all I wanted. Once I left, I assume the entire city, including a few neighboring towns, were informed of my banishment. And, to make matters worse, word got out about the death of Lynn, which a few months later would lead to the death of my beloved wife. See? I told you there was some structure left to my imagination.

So, yes, I will leave sooner rather than later. I will return to the ruins of Avalon, call out what now keeps me safe and ask it to leave. And once again, this is a battle I must fight alone, unfortunately. If, of course, it doesn't go quietly. It'll be Monday or Tuesday night, not sure how long I'll be away this time. Wish me luck, aye?

Monday, January 28, 2008

The Impending Fall Part VIII: Side A: The Unwanted

Perched quietly atop a crumbling rooftop of one of the few remaining buildings in the center of the city, it waited for me with its eyes glazed over in a cloud of determination.

When the mirror had shattered, random sections of the city crumbled to the ground, destroying the foundation of my imagination. The mark I bore on my wrist pulsed a gentle pigment of blue as the shadows of the darker recesses of my imagination collected at my feet, my irises fading to a gentle hue of what human's like to call "Ice Blue," a trademark sign of elemental mages plunging softly into the human emotion known as rage. I was no longer there to listen

179

to its lullaby.

In a distant echo, the soft sweetness of feminine laughter could be heard rippling through the darkness of the ruins of Avalon.

"You can confront me fiend, I'm not here to fight you." With a smile, I stopped short of the obliterated fountain that set itself in one of the alley walls. The echoes of the woman's laughter were heard again off in the distance as a calm shadow passed overhead and a figure landed next to me. Its hair was dark down to its shoulders, strait and soft with a gentle part to the right side. Blinking once, her irises faded from their brilliant golden hue to a soft blue, resembling that of a frozen afternoon summer sky. She smiled softly, placing a hand on my shoulder as my gaze shifted to her eyes.

"Cort, you finally came back. I've been waiting

for months for you to return."

"Yes, I'm sure you have. If you'd kindly leave now that I have returned and give the lullaby back to whomever you stole it from, that'd be wonderful."

"What's the matter, Love? I thought I was doing you quite a favor keeping you asleep at night."

"Swallow your tongue demon, I will kill you where you stand. And get rid of that costume you're hiding in. You will never become her." I laughed quietly at its failed attempt to mimic the physical memory of my wife as it let out a shrill cry of amusement, much like a siren in the dead of night laughing at the moon.

"Your courage makes me laugh, mage." Its voice had shifted slightly, still feminine, but slightly more demonic than before. Smiling again, it wavered from my sight.

"Go on, run, though shattered this is still my city." Blinking softly, I sat against the fountain as it began to rain, and flashes of lightning in the hollow sky bounced reflections off the window of a nearby building just outside the street I stood in, smiling as the rain soaked my hair, a few drops crawling down my cheek, falling like tears to the shadows at my feet. "I'm only going to say this once." I was screaming softly through the conjured rain with a surprisingly darker smile than I had expected to produce. "Leave me alone. I don't need your aide with sleep anymore." Again, the mocking cackle echoed through the conjured storm as the demon phased into existence in front of me with the playful smile of a jester stretched across its face.

"I'm not ready to leave to leave yet, Cort." I had to laugh at the remark, bowing my head in a gesture of false acceptance to its statement.

"Are all demons as deaf and stupid as you?" As I blinked again, its appearance change, to now fully resemble every aspect of my wife as it took me in its arms and began to whisper in my ear.

"Ziiju nil riem yu. Ziiju nil fierria." With a gloss of rage attached to my eyes, I grasped it around the throat, blinking in its direction as its shadow began to waver softly at its feet. For those that remember seeing this, I know I've yet to give a translation.

Directly pulled from the night Yari and I were married, "Sleep well my angel, sleep well tonight." A line from her drawn out speech about how happy she was that she could finally call me hers. It was quite adorable, I must admit.

Pulling the outsider closer to me, I smiled softly against its neck. "Don't say that ever again." It was then that any expression it may have possessed during the night was wiped from its face, and the frost of determination laced its bright golden eyes. Releasing my grip around it's throat, I smiled, amused at the sight of it's disgust with my defiance as it lunged at me, forcing me to the ground, screaming in rage as it began clawing at my body in attempt to tear me to shreds. Screaming violently, I winced as it tore flesh from my torso.

Wednesday, January 30, 2008

The Impending Fall Part VIII: Side B: Left for Dead

What would normally work on most barely phases that which I can't destroy. The Shadow crawling up its body wavered quietly as it screamed again, clawing at my neck. The remains of whatever human traits it hid behind started to fade as it blinked, backing away from my still corpse, giving me the chance to stand. I coughed silently as a smile crept across my face, staggering to my feet. "What would it take for you to leave now that I seem to have pissed you off?" I smiled again, managing to gain enough strength to stay on my feet.

It's only response was the same shrill cry it let out before, before fading from my sight again, appearing in front of me not seconds later with it's familiar

smile as it pounced on my chest, forcing me back

down on the ground, tilting it's head to the side as it's

hand slid softly around my throat, squeezing gently.

"Before I leave I might as well destroy you, since you

no longer want me around. I have no reason to be

around that which does not love me."

...

Before laying another hand on me it stopped,

looking up at the storm pouring down on us both,

standing over my still body.

"You're lucky, child..."

I was left alone, beaten once again to the brink of

life before it vanished for what seemed like for good.

Wednesday, March 19, 2008

It is you I have loved.

Seven years to the day mark the anniversary of our wedding, and I've spent five years without her...

Placed quietly under the fully bloomed rose tree rests the Staff of Ages, the useless weapon recovered from the ruins of the city I once called home. The weapon I thought could save her.

Seated at the edge of Urai, I tossed stones against the fetters of time in hopes she may throw one back to me, smiling at random memories as they flashed in my head.

You know...it's been so long I'm starting to forget what it feels like to have you around. Sad, I know, forgive me for that, but without your physical

187

body it's difficult to comprehend loving someone that actually exists. And yes, granted, I know you will tell me not to wait, to go find her, but where am I to look? Or perhaps, where am I to wait? For I wish to love you again...

Smiling gently, as seven diamond roses are cast to the wind, one for every year I have loved her.

For you, my Love, I would stop the world from ending. I would drown the sun in the shadow of the sky so that we may sleep next to each other a little while longer. If, in fact, the stolen lullaby I lost was yours, I wish to find it again. It kept me sane, and as such, the sanity your voice brought me kept my nightmares at bay.

Et din vacca ijulen ubae caar, imne hema dare oux ril kivie?...Mir nu rie oux ume fiil. Rie niec lou, seku din rana wem, heria vae yer rie juel ojorane, rie imne tev destrime... I know none of you have any clue what the previous text says, so here you go, the simplest of translations.

"If the world should end now, would she run to my arms?...Who am I to ask that. I love you, and when the day comes, that she and I are together, I will be complete."

April 3, 4, 14, 15, 2008

The Bloodline War Part I: A Love Worth Saving

When would it be justified to think revenge was the only option? Let me ask you this: if you watched the one you love die, and knew who was responsible, would you not feel compelled to destroy whoever took them away from you? Or perhaps if you could go back in time to save the one you love, what would stop you from doing so? If you remember the Staff of Ages and it's condition, its condition would be what's preventing me from saving her. But what if I could fix it? Replace the two shattered crystals with something else?

They've always been known as Necrien Crystals. The trinket that's been draped around the necks of visitors to aide them with breathing on Urai. If you were to take the crystal off it's chain and hold it up to the sun, you'd notice that it's cut the same way as the crystals that form the staff. Which is good news for me, right?

. . .

On a night where the roses on the tree are past the point of full bloom and every star in the sky has yet to show itself, I thought I was finally ready to attempt to get her back. All I could do was wait for the sun to come up, considering the night before I had reconstructed the staff, stringing two Necrien crystals in the places of those that had shattered months ago. And for those that aren't familiar with how the staff works, I'll give you a quick lesson on bending the flow of time. If you were to align the crystals with any line that resembles a horizon, in this case, the line where the sun crests the chasm on Urai, the crystals would align with the stars and take you wherever you wanted to go, though they were originally set in such a way that the staff would take the guardian back to the alter if she were ever to wonder off and happen to get lost. Think of it as a fail-safe, my brother and I built it that way just incase.

As the sun chases the shadows of space that lay quietly against the cliff side and the flowers in the field stand on end, eager to let the sun kiss their pedals, allowing them to flare one by one, once against setting the entire field ablaze. And, at the same time, the stars that hid from the sun as it rose to greet the field, blinked quietly into existence, lighting the abyss surrounding Urai with a soft white hue. Aligning the staff with one of the horizons of Urai, I smiled knowing it was finally time, and right before blinking out of existence the first two of three dominant symptoms of this method of time travel came over my body, the first being the feeling of "sea legs," though shrouded by and form of water, and the second a slight headache, much like a rush of blood to the head. Blinking out of existence, the remains of the unwanted element made a failed attempt to chase after me as I disappeared.

.   .   .

And, just like that, I was home. Welcomed by the scent of the air just before a rainstorm on a spring afternoon. The final side effect of this form of time travel, one of the more pleasant side effects of time travel if you ask me. When you tear a hold in the fabric of time, and walk backward to a previous memory, the soft sound of a dying storm surrounds the area you enter, causing a bit of ruckus is to be expected when using the staff. Shaking stardust from my hair as the scent of the prelude to a rainstorm subsided, I rose from one knee to my feet, only to be confronted by a smile I had missed for ages.

"What in the name of…C..Cort?" All she could do was stand there a bit stunned as to why I was home so early, and, with a quick smile, I wrapped her in my arms, not wanting to explain why I had come back when I did, and with the staff in hand of all things. "Baby, what are you doing here? Weren't you going to be on Urai for another week? And, what did you do to that staff of yours? Did something happen to you?"

Smiling, I shook my head, embracing her again as if I hadn't seen her in years…go figure, right?

"I'll tell you all about …" Then came the knock at the door, the knock at the door that defined the reason why I came back. "Let me get that, Angel." She smiled, and shook her head walking back downstairs to answer the door. "Yari, don't!" Chasing after her down the stairs, we both stopped at the door at the same time, as our eyes met for the first time in seven years. I had to smile and hug her again, whispering quietly in her ear ignoring the persistent knock at the door. "Rie niec lou, riem yu oux Terra." Blinking softly, the door opened just a crack as Yari poked her head outside first.

"Can I…can I help you gentlemen?" A bit startled by the memory of the key that swung quietly around my neck as I stepped up behind her, I removed it and dropped it in her hand, hoping it would trigger a memory and she would back away.

"We're here on Lady Taenvir's behalf, just looking for those that were associated with the one known as Ms. Lynn Winter." With a smile, she wrapped her hand around the key, opening the door the rest of the way. As she wrapped her hand around the key, she stepped back, again a bit startled as to why I had given her the key she knew I had no idea existed.

"Cort how did you?" With a smile, I bowed gently to the armed soldiers at in the doorway.

"Afternoon gentlemen, how may I help you?"

"We're looking for Cort Taenvir. Would you be him?"

"Aye, that'd be me, I'm the one who worked directly with Lynn, how can I help you?"

Yari poked her head next to me, startled. "Cort, what are you doing? Where are you going? Don't you dare leave me!" With a smile, I turned to her, taking her in my arms. "Take the girls and follow me to see Cara. I'll need the four of you there with me." With that, I followed the soldiers back to the heart of Avalon to confront my mother about the disappearance of my assistant, Lynn Winter, Yari and my daughters would soon arrive in the grand hall, as requested. So far, my Love was safe.

The Bloodline War Part II: Revenge on the Past May 15, 16, 2008 and other dates I can't remember.

How far would you go to save the life of the one you love, far enough that you would find a way to alter the flow of time and change the course of events in such a way that you would take their place?

Knowing the trial would end in violence, I opted to enlist help from the outside, enlist the aide of a walker with war-hardened branches of his imagination, and what we'll call a mage for now, one that, like myself, specializes in various branches of shadow manipulation at his disposal, along with my wife and three daughters, who followed me to the Great Hall the day Cara's generals came to the door.

The Grand Hall was built much like a church, a slightly elevated "stage" at the front of the building housed my mother and the members of the council with yours truly bound to the wall off to the right of the council. And, in front of us, multitudes of rows to the back of the Great Hall where ten more rows on either side of the building branched out like wings framing the only doors in or out of the building. Above the ten rows, rests an observer's balcony that seats roughly two hundred fifty people. Seated in the front row of the balcony were the members of my immediate family and two students of mine from years ago who had since become close friends of the family.

. . .

Raise your hand in the right manner of commanding silence and you'll one day hold the power to control the lives of anyone you want. Take that last statement with a grain of salt if you would, for you won't be able to walk into a room full of mindless, soul-sucking zombies, raise your hand and expect them to stop feeding just to hear what you have to say? Though why you would ever compare a room full of well-respected High Mages to hordes of mindless, soul-sucking zombies, raise your hand and expect them to stop feeding just to hear what you have to say. Though why you would ever compare a room full of mages to hordes of mindless, soul-sucking zombies is beyond me, but if you ever choose to, that might be what it looks like in your head.

It was then that a whispering silence fell over the masses in the Great Hall. Cara spoke firmly as she stood from her seat.

"Cort Taenvir, you've come of your own free will, confessing to the death of your assistant Lynn Winter?"

"No need for formalities Cara, everyone in this room knows our relationship. And, yes, I'm taking the blame for my experiment, as if anyone else would take the blame for me."

Mykel Starcatcher, standing 5'10 dressed in what could only be described as royal finery, black and deep blue chased in molten silver and flecked with shards of obsidian woven in to the fabric had black medium length hair and dark blue eyes beset a darkly, never-ageing, handsome face. Three swords accent his person, one long sword at each hip, and a two-handed broad sword upon his back, shifted quietly against the wall he leaned upon as he glanced over the opposition below the observer's balcony. Looking up at the front of the balcony, Cara shot a wicked smile at my wife as she continued to speak.

"Cort, as you already know, the punishment for admitting to such crimes, if found guilty, is death."

"Aye, a death similar to the death of my assistant, no doubt."

"I'm assuming you know what it feels like?"

"No, not really, it's not something I'd want to sign up for." I smiled in a joking manner.

"Mind your tongue child, or I'll force your daughter to perform your execution instead of the two I had already picked to kill you."

Struggling softly, I bit my tongue, refraining from snapping back at her as Setkai rose to her feet in a soft rage and began to speak. "Rie imne ishiizoria lou. Lou zotsaiku vorden."

Glancing up to the observer's balcony, Cara stood from her seat with a soft, twisted smile on her face. "Take your seat young one…or I'll have you restrained as well." Yari quickly pulled

Setkai back into her seat, whispering words of patience into her ear.

"Cort Taenvir, you are hearby deemed guilty of the following charges, treason, punishable by death, conspiracy against your people, punishable by death, avoiding authorities, punishable by confinement, overruled by the council as punishable by death, and finally, breaking laws of banishment, punishable by death. How do you plea?"

"Guilty to all charges."

Yari stood up this time, faster than I've ever seen any person move in all my years of living. "Cort, don't be a fool! You know you weren't the only one that worked on that project."

"Aye, I wasn't the only one, but I am its creator and, as such, the only one that should take the blame."

Yari slammed her fist against the railing of the observer's balcony. "Damnit Cort, I won't lose you again, you stubborn fool. I should be up there with you."

With a smile, I hung my head, staring blankly at the floor. "Don't you start talking like that, I came back to save you from a fate such as this…" Kelethin Blaad took a seat behind Yari and waited for a break in the conversation before putting his hand on her shoulder as tears fell from her eyes and she took her seat. Fierce and fiery green eyes full of youthful exuberance beset an average looking face topped with short-cropped sandy hair and matched with a similarly short-cropped goatee. 5' 5" and medium framed, barbed in soft leather armor with crossed baldrics holding twin kriss blades on his back, this youth of 18 looked rash and undisciplined, but by even merely watching his movements for a few moments, the trained eye will see what mere appearances deceive. Training since age four with the very same blades that adorned his back, no mere weapons are they, but just as much a part of him as his arms that wield them. His stance and walk, that of a man who lived every day from birth till this moment in a mercenary army. "Besides Love, I told you before, I won't…"

"Enough!" Cara's fists slammed in the pristine, white-marble table as she stood from her seat, growing impatient. "The two of you will swallow your tongues or I will be for to hold your entire family in contempt." The familiar silence I've grown accustomed to swept through the building as Cara took her seat and the trial continued. "To be perfectly honest, Cort, I can't imagine you'd want that, having been away from your wife for so long."

Struggling softly against multiple protests that ran through my head, the rush of helplessness came over me like a waterfall and a darkness fell over my eyes as the hollow plea of a forgotten memory returned for a few seconds before Cara's voice breached the walls of my imagination as I shook my head in an attempt to bring myself back from the quiet darkness that surrounded almost every inch of my thoughts. I suppose, having not reviewed the changed of the reborn city with those that don't have access to my dreamscape and the way it flows, you'd never know what I walked into the day I returned. But you're all familiar with my method of time travel at this point, right? I returned to a past that never welcomed me when it was the present. On top of that, Cara has always had issues with Yari. She always thought of her as the one that would lead me to my downfall. Not to say that she demanded we not get married, but she never approved of the relationship. I started to zone in and out, staring at the floor as Cara went on with the trial. It was then I started to realize just how long it had been since I had seen the Avalon that used to be, the Avalon I used to be a part of. Ten years of thinking way too much for my own good brought me to this point. The trial continued to play out like the low hum of some large fan acting as the power source to my dreamscape. Unfortunately, there are no epically boring details of this "trial," as my mother called it, that I could relay back to you aside from what you've already been told, for shortly after Cara started to get fed up with dragging out the death of her "betrayer" of a son as she once put it, in a dream that I never documented because it wasn't really that important. But, if you must know, the term betrayer was used because Cara thought my marrying Yari, a human at the time, who dabbled in the art of white magic and had such

extensive military background because of who her

parents were, was given the task of commanding over

half of my father's army during the first War of

Mages. Her parents, Gerik and Fioru Manaka, were

joint generals during a war that happened long before

my father was drafted into the military after marrying

Cara. Unfortunately, the war was so small that no

one ever found any documentation of it. Apparently,

shortly after the war was over, Yari was born and put

up for adoption in Tameril. A few months after her

birth, her parents were assassinated by a woman we in

Avalon know only as Taris the Weaver. She was one

of Avalon's biggest threats many years ago. If any of

you remember Lucian Orune, he was one of the last

shadow weavers to ever come face to face with Taris

after she went insane and wanted every mage in

Avalon that practiced shadow magic of any kind

destroyed. Lucian and his love Niirumi were the only two that managed to escape from Avalon and hide for a number of months before Taris' armies hunted them down.

Zoning in and out every so often, I had lost track of time, but by the looks of things it was almost time. The high mages in attendance were getting anxious, rustling about in their seats as they whispered curses amongst themselves of the return of the banished one that couldn't make up his mind.

Cara rose to her feet with a gentle sigh, having gone through the obvious evidence and presented guilty plea of her son and all I could do was hang my head smiling softly at the surprise that awaited the entire room. My mother started to speak again, in a tone suitable for a pack of ravenous wolves, yet gentle enough for her to still assume the role of a mother. "Would Ethcenia Grad and a man whose name you've never heard (we've always just called him Isaac, though most of us believe he went by a less "common" name growing up; but you'd never know it without asking him. Isaac, like Ethcenia was never a member of my mother's council; however, he was believed to be Ethcenia's mentor while she studied elemental distortion. But so little is known about him that she could have come up with that fetish all on her own.) stepped forward. Isaac seemed to appear from nowhere, though even when he was younger he was known for his entrances.

Silently manifesting among the population of the observer's balcony, disappearing, then reappearing again before the long, white-marble table, he bowed before my mother. Ethcenia, whom you might remember, was the little blonde girl who bore a striking resemblance to Setkai. A messenger in the once ruined city of Avalon, who had held me in such high respect, would now be one of the ones to carry out my execution. Ironic, isn't it? I had hoped at this point that I might find a way to let her live, but it didn't look promising.   The shadows beneath the navy silk sheers that kept the sunlight in the room limited to hints of a row of stained glass windows that lined the walls of the Great Hall began crawling to the middle isle, collecting in the shape of what looked to resemble rose pedals that laid softly on a puddle of water as Ethcenia's hand breached the floor, crawling slowly upward as she lifted herself from her manifestation and rose to her feet. Shaking the shadowed rose pedals from her hair with the most gentle of smiles, she bowed to Cara and the rest of the council and took her place beside Isaac. How ironic that the girl who hand no quarrels with me would be one of the ones to see me destroyed. The pictures depicted in each of the windows of a vast afternoon

sky, the pearl stained-glass designed to represent

clouds moved quietly through the row of windows

and as the sun outside the building moved through the

sky during the course of the day, there was never a

need for candlelight to keep the room lit during the

day, and when night fell, the empty, silver candle

abras fixed below the row of windows quietly

illuminated themselves, emitting a soft golden hue

along the walls of the Great Hall.

Cara stood again. "If the two of you

would introduce yourself to the hall, we'll continue

the trial." She sat back down.

Isaac stepped forward with a stern

expression, bowing again to the council before

turning to the masses behind him. "I am Isaac,

Manipulator of shadows." Bowing, he stepped back,

letting Ethcenia take her turn as she followed Isaac's

lead, bowing again to the council before her then turning to face the masses as she bowed again.

"I am Ethcenia Grad, daughter of Evil Grad and Magraad Shin, master of elemental distortion, with a main focus on shadow and water manipulation." Bowing her head after her introduction, she took her place beside Isaac. You could hear a stir of echoed whispers among the high mages, talk of Isaac's apprentice, and how fast she picked up on his teachings. I smiled quietly to myself, looking up at my wife. Starcatcher had moved from his seat in the back corner of the balcony, sitting next to Setkai, the two whispering back and forth, Setkai nodding twice. Cara's voice chimed in again.

"Cort Taenvir, you are hereby sentenced to death for the murder of your assistant

Lynn Winter. Isaac, Ethcenia, if you'd make your preparations, we'll get started."

A quiet breeze drifted through the Great Hall, my gaze lifting to the observer's balcony, as I smiled at Yari and the girls, watching the two elementalists take their positions in front of me. Starcatcher had once again moved to his comfortable leaning position, propped up neatly against the back wall, giving him access to the railing and a slight drop, exposing the top corner of one of the exit doors. Both Isaac and Ethcenia rose from their seats, their hands already having obtained the gentle shadowed hue; they stood in front of me, Ethcenia smiled softly at me. "It's good to finally meet you, Cort, my mother's told me so much about you."

I smiled at her, lifting my gaze to meet her own. "Gee, where have I heard that before? You really don't want to go through with this, child. I didn't mean for you to be one of the ones I would have to kill."

She tilted her head, a bit perplexed at my response as Isaac appeared next to her to make his introduction. "Greetings, Cort, I am Isaac, son of Acliician."

Yes, I know, you've never seen that name before. To be honest, this is the first time I've heard of it as well. "Acliician?"

"My father was one of the greatest shadow weavers to ever live…One day I'll take that title from him."

Ethcenia eye'd her hands with a soft smile as her gaze lifted to meet her mentor's. "It's time. Isaac, are you ready?"

"Yes indeed." He looked down at his hands, his fingertips a slightly darker hue than Ethcenia's. I struggled a bit in anticipation. It was almost time.

The Bloodline War Part III: If Revenge was given a name.

"Do not go into battle unless you know you can win." The first of many lessons my mother taught me when I was younger. I should tell you, if I'm not prepared to win this battle I'm screwed indefinitely, so hopefully all goes well. Remember when I told you Trega went into hiding when he was old enough to learn about the disappearance of his father? And how he would hunt me down the day I would finally return to Avalon, even for a reason such as this? He didn't make one of those epic entries like the guy that shows up at the wedding just after the priest says, "Does anyone have any objections as to why these two should not be wed?" At that point; someone barges in from the back of the church apparently having heard every word the priest said

217

and starts raving about why they should marry whomever is in question. In my opinion, it would have been hilarious if he came strolling up the middle isle with the darkest of smiles on his face, but I think Starcatcher would have tried to kill him had he made entrance. As it turns out, Trega had been there the entire time, seated in the front row at the end by one of the windows. Now, my vision isn't that great to begin with, but you'd think I would have noticed if he had been there from the start. The only reason I saw him at all was because he bothered to stand up while Isaac and Ethcenia were making their preparations. But the kicker is, no one stopped him, like he wasn't even supposed to be there. The only two that seemed to notice him were myself after he bothered to move, and Isaac, who struggled quietly as Trega stepped in front of him and wrapped a stealthy hand around his throat. It was then I glanced over at the council, only to find Evil Grad with her head bowed slightly and her eyes closed, mumbling silently to herself. Remember when I told you female time mages were rare even for an imagination as vast as mine? Ethcenia's mother was the only one.

Isaac struggled again, turning his attention to Trega as his physical body faded from the building. No, Trega didn't kill him, just preceded to scare him off so that he could have a clear shot at my existence. Not that you'll ever get the chance to meet him, but Trega has a means of persuasion that could kill a man. As Evil shook her head softly, seeming to blink tears from her eyes, the flow of time shifting seamlessly back to normal. Trega with the darkest of smiles stood next to Ethcenia, his ice-blue eyes making daggers at me as he restrained himself from ending the life of the one he thought killed his father.

Cara stood from her seat. "Ethcenia, if your preparations are complete, please proceed with the execution." She sat back down.

Trega smiled wickedly as I struggled against my restraints, noticing Yari rise from her seat to make yet another protest. "Cara, I beg you, take me instead!" I immediately shot an evil glare in Cara's direction as Kelethin tried to pull Yari to her seat. Blinking, as tears fell from her eyes, Yari shook him off as a soft wicked smile crossed Cara's face. "Take your seat. I will not refrain from taking you up on that offer if you interrupt again."

Kelethin finally pulled Yari back into her seat, offering her a white, silk cloth to dry her eyes.

. . .

Do you know what it feels like? To have your shadow pulled from your body? What about panic? Do you know what that feels like? To have your heart pound out of your chest because you start to think you will helplessly lose what you strived to protect? Or even death, I can't say I know anyone that doesn't have even a minute fear of death.

Trega set his hands in from of him, his arms fully extended and his fingertips an even darker hue than Isaac's. Ethcenia, who was too young to understand what was going on, continued with the execution.

Garith Brin, seated next to Kelethin, blinked and said nothing as the trial continued. Slightly graying hair and crystal blue eyes that bore the weight of over thirty years of commanding troops as both a general and a marshal adorn a face beginning to show signs of age and too many wars

221

fought. Crow's feet beside the eyes, frown lines cut the cheeks and a brow creased as though constantly calculating. Garith, standing 5' 8'' with chain mail nicked and scarred from countless battles but maintained with a practiced hand, a simple longsword at his side, wielded with the knowledge of survival against all odds. Garith turned to Kelethin after a few minutes whispering words of patience into the young warrior's ear as he saw his eyes widen when the execution started.

You don't notice it at first, when your shadow starts to gather at your feet. Though, if you were in any other situation than this, you'd wonder just what the hell was going on. But, if you were in any situation other than this, trust me, you'd probably want to run as fast as possible. No, I don't know what it feels like, not yet. This will be the first time I would have endured such a thing. Trega's smile grew a bit as my shadow wavered against the wall, and slid below my feet, crawling toward his hands. The next few minutes were a blur. I could feel my shadow start to pull gently against my body, slowly detaching itself. I screamed, struggling, which only made it worse. Ethcenia blinked as if unconscious, the shadow cast from my hands crawling along the floor toward her fingertips.

Trega's eyes flashed with a quiet hint of rage. "I will destroy you, mage. You will know what it feels like to lose what you love most, just as I did when I learned of my father's death."

I screamed again, struggling against my restraints, as a tall man of 6' 8'' with silvery eyes and short blond hair, clad in a gleaming breastplate, wielding a flaming flamberge stood from his seat at the back of the gallery to confront Starcatcher.

"Mykel, why are we waiting?"

Starcatcher smiled. "He can take care of himself still, just be patient."

The tall man, known simply as Guardian, ruffled his white feathered wings and stood beside Starcatcher, watching as the execution continued. Kelethin's eyes fixed on the ordeal. The twins now trying to hold Yari back from lunging at the two that were destroying her beloved husband. I screamed again, struggling to prevent the seemingly inevitable, making an attempt to save my own life as I made eye contact with both of my tormentors, watching as Ethcenia's shadow stirred beneath her, crawling silently up her feet and ankles. As the floor beneath her began to devour her limb by limb, her mother stood from her seat behind the marble table, waving a soft hand at her daughter as the familiar feeling of displacement swept through my dreamscape. She was trying to save her daughter. I smiled and tried my hand at drowning Trega as well, but he had caught on faster than Ethcenia, and already my shadow was manipulated in such a way that it started devouring me slowly as if to prolong an inevitable doom.

I screamed again in agony as my own shadow tore at my skin while crawling away from my body at the same time. Trega smiled again.

Tears fell from Yari's eyes as she spoke in confusion. "Why isn't he fighting back?"

As time slowed to a near stop, I felt my restraints shatter and then it was as if I blacked out for a few minutes, only to awaken again without them, Ethcenia's fingers breached the tile floor surrounded by the remains of her shadow. Evil was unable to save her daughter, so, instead, chose to save me. I shook my head and tried to get my bearings, as

I turned to face the one that had accused me of killing his father.

As the flow of time caught up with itself, the masses below the observer's balcony had stood slowly trying to comprehend what had happened.

The entire first row had turned their attention to myself and Trega, who, with rage in his eyes, had lunged at me, pinning me to the ground, shouting threats while removing a dagger the size of a letter opener from a sheath at his thigh, jamming it forcefully into my shoulder. Starcatcher smiled gently at Guardian. "Now, it's time."

Nodding slightly, Guardian kicked off the back wall of the observers balcony, spreading his wings to full extension, sailing over the length of the hall, to land a few feet in front of and between the front rows, flaring his wings upon landing.

Tilting her head to the side in confusion, an angered scowl crossed her face as she eyed the observer's balcony. I had brought help she never saw coming. I told you I would come at her from above, did I not?

As she scanned the observer's balcony, her angered scowl turned to a smug smile, amused by her son's so called "help." Maraud and Evil eyed Cara who, as they stood, calmly motioned for them to take their seats again. "No need to move, they are of no threat to us."

The High Mages of Avalon seated on either side of the building rose to their feet and started to pour from the pews, making an advance on the newcomer. Standing from her seat, Yari motioned to her daughters, Setkai's eyes fixed on Cara. One by one, Yari, our children and both Gareth and Kelethin jumped from the railing of the balcony, standing slowly to face the rows of mages seated in the wings of rows at the back of the Hall. Turning their attention to the six of them, the middle isle started to fill with a blockade of mages as Gareth and Kelethin flanked either side of the middle isle giving Yari and the girls a chance to advance up the middle isle. Setkai stood in front of Yari with a wicked smile. "Let me take care of Cara…"

Turning her back to her mother and sisters, she started to walk forward, her iris's fading to the color of the midnight sky. As she passed the rows of High Mages, making her way to the front of the Grand Hall, you could hear the screams of high mages, clutching their temples as they collapsed, convulsing violently on the floor.

Smiling through the pain, I looked Trega in the eye, removing the dagger from my shoulder. "If only you knew the truth. I never killed Dunel, he left of his own accord years before you were born." Blinking softly, Trega's shadow began to waver, crawling up his arm.

"Liar!" Standing, Trega lifted his palm to the ceiling as I rose from my position on the floor and was flung into one of the marble columns behind me, the crack in the column lightly rupturing the foundation of the ceiling. Dust and marble fell to the floor as I shook my head. Trega's dagger had fallen from my hand and lay as if neatly placed point side down, splintering the marble on the corner of the table.

Turning their attention to the screaming masses behind them, the high mages funneling from the pews on the floor stopped their forward advance on the single threat standing between Guardian and the council. With their attention turned away, Guardian launched himself forward into the midst of the high mages. With Guardian's first violent swing of his flaming flamberge, six mages were felled, their bodies tossed into the air like rag dolls, their robes instantly igniting. Guardian's smile widened as he began plowing his way through the center of the mass of high mages, sending flaming bodies left and right, some landing back into the pews from whence they came. The high mages turned their attention back to Guardian, confusion and a tinge of fear on their face, as they stood almost rooted at the horror of watching their members being torn apart with such apparent ease.

Hope and Faith stood quietly next to Yari, their fingertips gaining a soft blue hue. Icicles hung silently from the ceiling, Faith, waving her hand at the masses in front of the three of them with a smile, brought the conjured frost down from the Heavens impaling high mages at random as they made their way to the front of the building. Hope smiled as the impaled mages let out screams of pain, and waved her hand at the second row of their opposition, dropping to one knee she set her finger on the floor, as icy veins shot from her fingertips and started crawling to the rest of the high mages standing in the middle isle. Now immobile, the mass of high mages began conjuring various branches of elemental magic through their hands, glowing a different hue ranging from a darker shadow to a brilliant white.

Noticing the high mages beginning to fight back, Starcatcher smiled slightly as he teleported to stand before the front doors. "My turn." Crossing his arms, Starcatcher began to counter the energies that the high mages were summoning. One by one, the high mages glowing hands winked out, like the light of candles being quickly snuffed by a strong wind.

With the distraction in place, Yari took this opportunity to silently make her way around the back of the stadium style pews to the front of the Grand Hall. "Let my husband go." Disappearing while running to the front of the Grand Hall, Yari reappeared a few feet behind Trega, folding her hands in front of her chest, a glowing aura surrounding her hands. Standing, I smiled at Yari, turning my attention back to Trega as my wounds started to heal themselves.

Her hands clenched softly in fists of rage, Setkai started to make her way to the marble table at the front of the building, passing the charred corpses that lined the center isle. As she passed Guardian, as soft smile crossed her face, noticing Kelethin following her a few steps behind. Guardian made his way to the back of the Grand Hall, Magraad and Evil stood from their seats backing away from Setkai as she made her advance toward Cara. Setkai stopped a few feet short of the marble table. Magraad and Evil, both fear-stricken, backed into the wall behind them and wavered through the stone, disappearing to leave Cara to fend for herself.

"Leave my family alone, witch. I will make you suffer beyond your wildest dreams. There will be no coming back from this." The familiar darkness that clouded Setkai's eyes resonated from her body as she rose serenely off the floor and Cara stood to face her with runes manifesting over her shoulders and in front of her palms. "I wouldn't try to save yourself. I should tell you now, nothing you have in your possession will ever stand a chance against me." Setkai smiled, blinking softly as Cara clenched her fists, collapsing over the marble table, screaming at the top of her lungs, her irises fading from her eyes as she continued screaming. And, when it was over, the echo of my mother's screams seemed as though they could be heard for miles. Shaking the shadows from her eyes, Setkai winced as if recovering from a brain freeze, dropping to the floor to rest a moment.

Kelethin glanced back at the screaming, seeing that Setkai had things well in hand, he turned his attention back to the mass of high mages now recovering from their attempted spells being summarily cut off. Kelethin smiled as he twirled his dual kriss blades, slowly advancing towards the high mages. Upon reaching the first of the high mages Kelethin leaped into action, flashing from high mage to high mage as though he was teleporting, slicing through them with ease. The unarmed and unarmored high mages stood little chance against what would best be described as a whirling dervish of blades and speed that had been let loose on their ranks, falling to the speed and ferocity of Kelethin's blades in such quick succession that it appeared as if the high mages were mere dominos that Kelethin had knocked over. One by one, the high mages fell, Kelethin moving swiftly and effortlessly from one to the other, jumping, flipping, kicking, twisting and weaving death with each passing moment.

In the middle of battle, a person becomes focused on what is in front of them or near them, their sense of hearing drowned out by the clash of battle. Only a trained veteran of countless wars could focus past that, only one so used to the sounds of death happing in the great hall could hear the low dull thud of the great doors as an army of troops were attempting to break in. Starcatcher heard the dull thud and turned to face the doors, shaking his head slightly. "The arrogance of these mortals thinking that could have any impact on the outcome of this." Raising his hands slightly, Starcatcher motioned towards the doors, blowing them out towards the army trying to enter. The doors sheared off their hinges, being forced in a direction they were never meant to go, plowing through hundreds of troops in an instant, and coming to rest a few hundred feet away from the great hall. Slowly walking out from the great hall, Starcatcher observed the remains of the troops assembled. Shaken and disorientated, the troops could only stare at Starcatcher as he shook his head in apparent disapproval and rose his hands again. The troops were hit without warning and without a means to defend themselves from the onslaught of magical energies that were unleashed upon them, some combusted igniting and incinerating others near them, some shattered from extreme cold sending shards of frozen flesh into their nearby comrades. The majority of the troops were slain by mini black suns that darted around the battlefield shredding away the thin connection that a mortal's soul possesses with its body. In mere moments, Starcatcher had decimated the army, the tattered and frightened remnants fleeing in sheer terror at the atrocities that they had witnessed. Smiling slightly, Starcatcher let them flee. Turning back to the Grand

Hall, he walked in to observe as the last of the high mages fell.

"Trega, there is no hope for you. I will explain this one last time. Dunel left of his own accord years ago. I haven't heard from him since. There was no killing involved, can't you see that?" Trega threw Yari against one of the windows as he charged at me again. "Swallow your tongue, mage…I don't believe you!"

Shaking my head in his direction, I caught his wrist as he dove toward me, flipping him into the already cracked pillar behind me. Wrapping my hand into a fist, his shadow began to spiral up his legs, collecting in a small pool underneath him. With a glint of rage in my irises, I offered little mercy to the boy that would seemingly never see reason. Sinking faster into the marble floor, Yari stood next to me, watching as the boy who tried to kill her husband was being devoured just as I was. "Cort, where did you learn to do this?" A puzzled look crossed her face as she shifted her gaze back and forth from Trega to me.

"It's been years since I have seen you, my Love. The staff is in its current condition because I had to fix it to save you from this very fate. Had I not been there to answer the door, you would have died in those shackles. And I told you, I won't lose you again."

Trega's screams echoed through the recesses of the Grand Hall. Bones cracked under the pressure of darkness as I tried my best not to smile at my victory. With Trega gone, I released the tension in my fists, my hands shaking just enough to be noticed.

"Cort, it's okay. It's over." I smiled at her. For the first time in five years, I had held the one I called my own. It seemed to be over. At least for the time being, for when the echoes of Trega's screams had died down, from the shadows of the observer's balcony emerged a boy. A boy I had seen before, enveloped in shadows. From there, he vanished, appearing in front of me not seconds later with a smile of hope stretched across his face.

"I am Zelthin, son of Durah. I seek your help in finding Shorova, and your daughter has someone here to see her." Pointing to the back of the Hall, I followed his gesture, only to see a woman standing in the doorway, a woman of more years than any one of my family members had seen. "I believe you two already know each other, Cort."

I looked at the boy as the woman standing in the doorway made her way to the front of the hall. Her dark hair brushed quietly against her shoulders as she confronted me, bowing with a smile. "

"It's been too long, Cort. I see my son finally found you."

I smiled. "Stubborn fool almost killed me. Didn't you tell him?"

"He didn't listen to me, did he listen to you?"

Shaking my head I hugged the newcomer. "Not at all. Yari, meet Charlotte, an old friend of the family and, even closer friend to Dunel."

Bowing, Yari wrapped the woman in a hug. "I'm sorry for your loss. Dunel was a good man."

Charlotte smiled and returned Yari's hug, glancing over at Setkai who had taken an interest in her a few minutes ago, staring in confusion as if she knew her from a past she couldn't remember. Tapping me on the shoulder, Setkai cleared her throat and began to speak. "Ahem…Cort, who is she?"

Charlotte smiled at her. "You wouldn't remember me. It's been ages. My name is Charlotte Hemlocke, and I've come to take you home."

I looked at her, puzzled and confused. "Wait, what? Charlotte, why would you want to take Setkai home with you?"

She smiled. "She's my sister, that's why. Sweetie, your real name is Aurora Hemlocke, you're the second youngest of five sisters adopted by a scientist, Alaster Hemlocke. That ability you have? We all have something like it. It's what Xander was trying to cure before he passed away. You, however, were given up for adoption again shortly after you turned three, and brought here to keep you under control."

"Control? I don't wish to hurt anyone."

Hugging Aurora, Charlotte laughed. "I know, Love. I'll explain everything when we get home.

Cort, I'm grateful for what you've done. Thank you from the bottom of my heart for looking after my sister. My apologies again for any damage Trega might have done."

"Don't worry, love. It's over now. I think, however, that Zelthin here might need a little guidance. Yari, what say we take him home and hear his story?"

Yari smiled, throwing her arms around me. "Why not just stay here? We belong here."

I nodded and smiled gently in Starcatcher's direction. "How can I ever thank you for what you've done?"

Smiling down at me, the others joined Starcatcher at his side. "No need to thank us friend, it's what we do. I'll have your staff delivered to you at some point, don't worry." Gathering themselves,

Starcatcher and the others wandered out of the Great

Hall, seeming to vanish into thin air.

Epilogue

Journal Entry: 5/15/2011

Dream Entry: Scattered through-out the past two weeks

This was originally written in blue text, and that means they've started again.

I'm not sure if this entry even deserves a title, as I wouldn't even begin to tell you that I know what to call it. It's been nearly two months, perhaps a bit longer, perhaps a bit less. Honestly I can't remember. And you'd think I'd remember such an iconic evening when Pandora was destroyed.

When these nightmares first started I was told simply to write them down. And that if I did, soon enough they would go away. Would you believe that I started writing them down in February of 2006? It's been too long.

People are funny. "What did you eat before you went to bed?" They ask me, as if what you eat before you go to bed has a remote effect on what you dream about or whether or not you have a nightmare. The hell does it matter? If I ate cookies shaped like Pandora, then it would make sense, would it not? But no, they don't make such baked goods, nor should they ever. Those that have never met Pandora, or have never read any of the entries would probably not find the following nightmare as frightening as I do, and for that I apologize for not being able to put in such a perspective that will make you understand how frightening the thought of her return is.

The nightmare itself is purely situational, and what I mean by that, is if I just stand there and do nothing, I'm safe. However, the minute I try to talk to her, or say anything at all, she simply smiles, blinks, and then screams at me. At which point I start to unravel like a sweater. It's painful, by any stretch of the imagination, let alone my own. A dear friend of mine told me not to think about her, for reincarnation was possible through thought. That alone is frightening enough. Hell, just that thought by itself is more frightening than the nightmare.

You might be thinking to yourself. "Just keep quiet and you won't die every time." While this logic is actually true, and quite full-proof as it's happened a few times out of the slightly less than numerous times that I've had the nightmare, as I said before, if I just stand there and say nothing, she just stands there and says nothing, only screaming at me when I attempt anything at all. And sure, there are a multitude of things I could do at the blink of an eye, for that's how things work now, sometimes even faster than that. But she's faster. And all I'm trying to do is figure out what she's doing here, if she's even actually here at all. "Come now, you're smart enough to know that when it fails and you are left alone, I will be the one to take from you that which you hold closest to your heart." Those words came from her mouth, not his. I need to fix this. But how do you fix that which makes no sense. Here's to hoping she's just a dream.

Journal Date 9-1-2011

I know it has been a while since her name has been mentioned. Months after learning what she was, I wracked my brain to try and figure out a way to kill that which according to those that know anything there is to know about demons and the like is that they unfortunately cannot die. So, the question was raised years ago, "How do you kill that which does not die?"

It occurred to me years later, that while I wasn't strong enough to destroy Pandora, I knew of two that were more than willing to do away with her. It made things a lot easier. There isn't much to tell, really. I was asleep when it happened, but it wasn't like your normal dream or nightmare. And I could try to explain to you how and where it happened, but most of you that read this, I imagine would look a bit

249

perplexed. By now, you're all familiar with Avalon and some of its intricacies. That's where it happened. Two on one. I imagine it was quicker than usual. My friends, the one's I let do away with Pandora, they move pretty fast. Example, think of a number between five and ten, or the sake of simplicity, think of the simplest thought you can, or the most complex, honestly it won't matter for explanation's sake. What I'm trying to get at is they move faster than the speed of light or sound. You may ask what travels faster than speed or sound. How easy was it for you to think of that number? Pretty simple, huh? Fast too, eh? The speed of thought probably isn't something you've heard mentioned before, that's okay, by now most things you've read revolve around things you aren't familiar with. Long story short, and lack of details about the epic battle aside, Pandora is for all intents and purposes, dead. I use the term "dead" very loosely, however, I suppose "gone" would better suit the situation, given as I said before, they can't die per-se, having said that though, she is no more.

Thank you,

I thought it best to let you all know that I love you and can't thank you enough for everything you've done.

::Lindsley and Athyzil:: (my stronghold and guardian, I owe the both of you my life)

::Tracey Fida:: Thank you for editing the book, without your help, I would have never finished it.

::Miss Erica:: (The one that finally made me realize what the fuck I was doing to others, I love you, Angel)

::Think:: (my therapist, you my friend are one of a kind)

::Rowmeo:: (The one that refused to lose me, I owe you more than you can imagine)

::Alana:: (For not throwing me into the vacuum of space. I would not be where I am now without you.)

::Charlie:: (the one that told me to keep writing, I'm glad I listened to you, boss.)

::Elly:: (for making me smile even when things didn't look so good.)

::Jillbean:: (The one always willing to listen. Thanks for making me smile.)

::Christina:: (For walking through Hell and back with me, willing to hold my hand through it all. You my dear, I can't thank enough)

::Mike:: (The brother I never had. Thanks for looking out for me, bro.)

::Hope:: (You seemed to understand everything I told you. I love you, sweetie.)

::Jen-Jen:: (I know when you first heard this story you were a bit overwhelmed. Thanks for being there to listen though.)

::Kirsten:: (For believing in my ability to captivate an audience with my imagination, I hope one day you have the chance to read it.)

::Rose:: (For being there when I needed you.)

::My Parents:: (For drilling the notion of control into my head.)

::Katie:: (For taking the time to listen, and offering advice when needed. Had it not been for you, I don't think I would have ever been able to get this far in the book.)

::Cody:: (Love you like a brother, boss. No doubt. Thanks for the hugs, and advice)

::Julia:: (For my memory retention. The work you've helped with is beautiful and I can't thank you enough Thank you for listening and being among the handful that told me not to give up.)

::Shey:: (I've never actually seen Urai until the day you drew it for me. Thank you for helping me put my imagination on paper.)

::Kevin:: (For the artwork. It's still amazing. I can't thank you enough.

::Ben:: (For the artwork. Among my most cherished pieces)

::Karel:: (For the artwork. Miss you man, hope everything is well.)

::H Lovey:: (While you might refer to me as your hero, you and yours are my hero's. You've helped me more than you might know. Love your face.)

::Jill:: (For being among the handful that told me not to give up.))

::Heather Marie:: (For pushing me to finish the book. Love you.)

::Joe Mccarthy:: You have helped me with so much, I won't list everything here. Thank you for the orchestration, for the support, and most of all for being there when it counted most.

To those I may have missed in a personal thank you, this does not mean that I'm not thankful for you; it just means it is late and my memory is failing me. Thank you all for everything you've done for me, be it big or small, it was something amazing.

www.ingramcontent.com/pod-product-compliance
Lightning Source LLC
Chambersburg PA
CBHW070837280626
47161CB00015B/1025